CHRIST'S ENTRY INTO BRUSSELS

Born in Belgium in 1972, DIMITRI VERHULST is the author of a collection of short stories, a volume of poetry and several novels, including *The Misfortunates* and *Madame Verona Comes Down the Hill*, published by Portobello Books. In 2009 he was awarded the Libris Prize in the Netherlands.

DAVID COLMER is a multi-award-winning translator whose work includes books by Cees Nooteboom, Gerbrand Bakker, Annie M.G. Schmidt and the cartoonist Gummbah. He is the recipient of the NSW Premier's Translation Prize, the Independent Foreign Fiction Prize and an IMPAC-Dublin Literary Award. In 2012 he was awarded the Dutch Foundation for Literature prize for lifetime achievement in translation.

D1342124

700041175143

ALSO BY DIMITRI VERHULST
FROM PORTOBELLO BOOKS

Madame Verona Comes Down the Hill
The Misfortunates

Christ's Entry into Brussels

(In the year 2000 and something,
or thereabouts)

DIMITRI VERHULST

Translated from the Dutch by David Colmer

Portobello
BOOKS

Published by Portobello Books 2014

Portobello Books
12 Addison Avenue
London
W11 4QR

Copyright © Dimitri Verhulst, 2011

English translation copyright © David Colmer, 2014

Originally published in Dutch in 2011 as *De intrede
van Christus in Brussel (in het jaar 2000 en oneffen ongeveer)*
by Uitgeverij Contact, Amsterdam.

The translation of this book is funded by the Flemish Literature
Fund (Vlaams Fonds voor de Letteren – www.flemishliterature.be).

Flemish
Literature
Fund

A CIP catalogue record for this book is available
from the British Library

2 4 6 8 9 7 5 3 1

ISBN 978 1 84627 467 1

Typeset in Bembo by Patty Rennie
Printed in the UK by CPI Group (UK) Ltd, Croydon CR0 4YY

www.portobellobooks.com

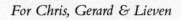

For Chris, Gerard & Lieven

La la la lala la la la la la la
lalala lalala la la la la la la

First Station

People claim that starting a story with a description of the weather shows a distinct lack of craft and I see where they're coming from. But that doesn't mean I have a better alternative – and believe me, I've considered them all – than opening this account by stating that it was not raining on the morning of the day on which it was announced that Christ would soon be visiting Brussels. It was more the nondescript kind of weather Belgium excels in, the weather that helps it maintain its position as a global leader in the consumption of antidepressants. It's a phenomenon that is more than familiar to anyone who's ever flown to our capital: fluffy, fleecy, candyfloss clouds clumping together the moment you enter our air space and darkening as the descent commences. Thick and gloomy, they gather over the runway, and the first sight of that mass of cloud is generally enough to drain any batteries the homecoming passengers have recharged over the course of their holiday. The rattling aircraft drills a path through the thick mists, a voice pants *à la française* that it's time to fasten your seatbelts, and a different voice says the same thing in no-nonsense Dutch while straining to conceal a Leuven accent. Weeks of constant rain is the only realistic expectation and it's always surprising how low you've already sunk when you finally see the ground, how much detail you can make out as you study the lawns on which trampolines stand next to big, blue, unused soup bowls of swimming pools, the square middle-class villas lining the roads, the neatly trimmed hedges surrounding the houses, the neighbourhoods in which alarm systems protect children and chattels. But, no . . . it's not raining. It's neither hot nor cold, grey nor blue, and definitely not one of the two hundred annual days of precipitation that fans of averages are so fond of quoting. The wind is blowing from where it generally blows from , the southwest, nowhere near strong, but with just enough force to convince lazy cyclists to subject themselves to the misery of public transport.

That was the kind of weather on that particular morning, and predicting it would have been a cinch. It wasn't raining – I'm happy to repeat that – not in the slightest, not a single stray drop was falling from the sky. And because the inhabitants of this kingdom value the anonymity provided so perfectly by an umbrella, it was up to them to *imagine* their umbrellas: cocoons, psychological demarcations, walls separating them one from the other to make sure there was no need for contact. Fashionable tracksuits were kitted out with cowls the young were only too keen to use, drawing their whole troublesome personality back out of sight or pushing the earphones of their MP3 players deeper into their ear-holes to shut out the ugly sounds of the world. On all lines, above and below ground, between Gare du Nord and Foyer Schaerbeekois, between Berchem Shopping and the Porte d'Anderlecht, between the stop for Montgomery and the stop for Gare de l'Ouest, everywhere, commuters were texting chit-chat somewhere else – the form of communication they hid behind to avoid conversation. Faces were buried in news-papers, noses turned towards windows, leaving damp spots behind on the glass. If not for the bell that rang to alert passengers to approaching stops and the occasional wild cry rising from a baby's buggy, there would have been nothing at all to distract the figures in this deaf-and-dumb tableau from their own ongoing funeral procession.

Those who believe there's no such thing as coincidence consider it prophetic that Pieter Bruegel the Elder, possibly the city's best-known son, nicknamed Peer the Turd, assured himself of a place in history by painting the most famous of all biblical towers. With its frustration at being hindered in all things by its mishmash of languages, Brussels had in any case been compared many times to the ziggurat of Babel. Inside its buildings, the inhabitants prayed, dreamt, threw plates and made love in every possible dialect from every corner of the globe. But on trams, trains and buses, they were all just languages to shut up in. And what few dared to admit was that most people were delighted to live in a place where humanity was present in all its diversity. It gave everyone with inborn antisocial tendencies a cheap excuse for hiding behind the façade of their mother tongue.

There was no point angling for a smile or a hello in the city centre, unless of course you were dealing with shop assistants who were willing to demean themselves with a touch of friendliness in an attempt to offload some summer stock that had already gone out of fashion. Haste and speed – whether more or less of either – were a barrier to any kind of politeness: the word 'please' was a waste of valuable time. People hoping to return home with their faces unscathed were better off assuming that nobody would be holding any doors open for them.

Back in front of their own flickering fireplace, these individuals slithered over to their computers, where they used pseudonyms to spew poison on all kinds of blogs. They spat in the face of entire communities, juggled obscenities and accompanied their foul-mouthed diatribes with threats aimed at those whose opinions were a consequence of actual thought. But in physically tangible reality, they were heads without speech bubbles, outstanding performers in their roles as silent extras in the metropolitan mass spectacle.

It wasn't raining, unless you went by people's faces. Drained and rained on, soaked and oafish every day.

The news of Christ's coming – and I, despite being averse to all persuasions, can only call it happy – reached most of us Belgians, bravest of all the Gauls, in the glass cathedrals of the central business district after we got bored with the umpteenth game of patience and surfed to a news site, frowning deeply and chewing the ends of our pencils in a pretence of concentration designed to mislead our heads of department. There it was, tucked away between an item about an attempt on the world hotdog-eating record and one listing the latest antics of a female pop singer. Christ was coming to Brussels on the twenty-first of July. Although anonymous, the sources were highly reliable and His coming was a definite fact. Further information would follow.

The serenity with which this item was both presented and read was as miraculous as its contents. True, society had secularised to its heart's content, but most people still had more faith in God than in journalism. The hacks had fewer and fewer scruples when it came to filling pages, columns were farmed out to celebrities with more fame than brain and, judging by the number of words, a TV quiz was considered more important than the suffering in places like Sudan. Journalists flaunted the term 'sexy', applying it to both politicians and shares. Editors did their moral duty by placing an article about ecological degradation in the news section, then filled the weekend supplement with praise for shamelessly fashionable trips to distant kerosene-guzzling paradises. If the newspaper grew tired of the real world, it commissioned a pollster to produce a statistic that conned the readers into believing that French-speaking Belgians spent more time in their kitchens than Dutch-speaking Belgians, vaguely insinuating that these were two completely different species with distinct DNA sequences and thought patterns. And even more pernicious for the reputations of the paper whistle-blowers was the indiscriminate way they swallowed and propagated so much guff. A young film-maker who was hungry for the attention of the public only needed to dispatch a press release that his latest cinematic effort had won the Golden Applause Meter at the renowned Sarajevo Film Festival and the next day the article would be picked up by fourteen independent and ostensibly critical papers. Clearly, we had no reason to get excited about the news of Christ's coming.

★

I can't remember anyone jumping up out of their office chair that afternoon. Nobody burst out laughing at reading something that could easily have been taken as an inspired joke; no religious souls crossed themselves; no cries of joy interrupted the harping song of the printers and photocopiers. And even the smokers – brought together by the Ministry of Health as the common enemy and forced to spend their breaks outside on public display as weak-willed objects of ridicule – kept this quite extraordinary fact out of their conversations. Of course, we had to leave the head of department under the illusion that we had busied ourselves exclusively with the details of invoices; we didn't want our salaries called into question. And it was also possible that we simply didn't believe our own eyes. Afraid of it being an unnoticed typo, we waited for someone more courageous to finally expose themselves to ridicule by saying, 'Hey, did you see that article, Jesus Christ . . .'

We all read the news alone and kept it to ourselves.

It *was* raining when we clocked off that evening. Quite heavily, in fact. But you wouldn't have known it from the way people were acting. Umbrellas remained unopened. Even adults were skipping from puddle to puddle. Drivers realised that they'd forgotten to beep their horns like idiots and had still managed to make it from one end of the Rue de la Loi to the other without picking up any fresh dents. On the tram a woman suddenly said, '*Nous sommes des passeurs, nous avons besoin de mots des autres,*' because she had just read it in her newspaper and found it so beautiful that she felt a need to say the whole sentence out loud. A very small part of her wanted, out of habit, to apologise for this impulsive act, but it was too late: she had broken through the commuters' lethargy with her words and she had enjoyed it.

For myself, I did something I hadn't done for ages and stopped in Les Jardins du Luxembourg to buy flowers for my wife, white ones. A whim that showed *me*, more than anyone else, that I was apparently still willing to work on stopping that sleepy marriage of ours from dozing off permanently.

Second Station

Belgium is one of the Holy Family's favourite travel destinations, always has been. Anyone who has combed through the archives of the Roman Curia can attest to that. Most notable was the dark year of 1933, when the Virgin Mary appeared on Belgian soil so often it must have been quiet up in Heaven. Just over forty days before the start of the calendar year, on the nineteenth of November 1932, She started Her run on top of the railway viaduct of Beauraing, beaming as if She'd knocked back a glass too many of Elixir d'Anvers, and aiming that somewhat sinister smile at five children of humble origins. Up to and including the third of January 1933, She would appear to these children no less than thirty times, standing beneath the branches of a hawthorn hedge. 'I am the Queen of Heaven,' the body in the radiant glow declaimed, 'Queen of Heaven and the Mother of God. Pray to Me! Pray always!' The news spread like syphilis and soon coaches headed for the mystical site were leaving Brussels, Charleroi, Givet, Dinant, Namur and St. Hubert. From all over the magnificent Gothic-novelist-favouring Ardennes, extra trains to Beauraing were scheduled so that all and sundry could witness the miracle. The children to whom the Mother of God had revealed Herself were observed by a range of psychiatrists, all of whom reached the independent conclusion that not one of the five had a screw loose. Completely normal children, touched by ecstasy. The people – having arrived en masse from all regions of the country with picnic baskets and rosary beads and warming themselves in their misery on this revival of religious mania – sang to the Madonna, '. . . extend Your blessed hand out over Belgium.'

Twelve days later and 85 kilometres down the road, in Banneux, a village whose only claim to fame prior to that day had been its colossal pies, the Blessed Virgin appeared again to another child, a girl called Mariette Beco, a semi-namesake, and led her to a trickling spring with the cryptic words, 'This spring is reserved for all nations – to relieve the sick.'

And Mary did extend Her blessed hand out over Belgium: in that same year the most famous of all mothers popped up in Herzele, Onkerzele, Etikhove, Olsene, Tubize, Wielsbeke, Wilrijk, Verviers, Berchem and Foy-Notre-Dame, unhindered by language boundaries and to the great merriment of building contractors, as every apparition was honoured by the immediate construction of a chapel. Many saw it all as proof of Mary's disinterest in geopolitics, because if there was anywhere She could have assisted mankind with Her apparitions in 1933, it was Germany, where a new Messiah had just arisen, one with less beard than his predecessor but a more neatly trimmed moustache.

The Blessed Virgin Mary: She'd been here so often, She probably knew Belgium better than She knew the Holy Land itself. *Hail Queen of Heaven, the ocean's tar . . . thrown on life's urge, we claim thy car.*

But 1933 wasn't the only year to feature disproportionately in God's mum's travel diary. In 1415 the devout peasants of Scherpenheuvel placed a statue of the Virgin Mary in a hollow oak. In the absence of reliable doctors, and still awaiting the invention of antibiotics, the local ague sufferers went there to pray, apparently with success. When a shepherd tried to steal the statue, he was immediately struck with paralysis and unable to move from the spot, as if frozen in place. It was only after the holy statue had been returned to the hollow that he could be liberated from his comic predicament. Later, in 1603, drops of blood rolled down over the lips of that same statue, a gruesome fact that was passed down to us by no less than three eye witnesses. Someone who wouldn't question a single comma in this story is Maria Linden, yet another namesake. In September 1982, this resident of the municipality of Maasmechelen noticed the plaster statues of Mary on her mantelpiece weeping tears of blood. The news crew from the national broadcaster arrived just a little too late to capture what would have been an international first.

But never before in our national history had we known the Mother of God to intervene as resolutely as She did in 1919 in Malmedy, where a man had forced his way into a lady's home with, as could be deduced from his already unbuttoned trousers, dishonourable intentions. The lady threatened to call upon the aid of the Holy Virgin if the undesired intruder did not cover up his privates and leave the house double-quick. And there can be no doubt that the rapist would have been tickled pink to hear his defenceless victim threatening him with a – ha-ha – virgin. Until the Alma Redemptoris Mater suddenly really was there, right next to the bed, completely fearless and lighting up the whole room so brightly with the glow of Her aureole that the poor sinner had no choice but to flee out into the night. According to some accounts he was afflicted with erectile dysfunction ever after. Hardly surprising.

★

But all these folkloric occasions involved visitations of Mary. Now we'd been promised the arrival of Jesus Christ himself, in person!!! And not just rocking up out of nowhere in some rural hole, no. *Preannounced*! And going straight to the capital! Which happened to also be the capital of Europe!

As relaxed and murmuring as the news – you could call it the Glad Tidings – had been that afternoon when it caught our attention, by evening it was raucous, a hubbub through every conversation. The TV networks, of course, weren't interested in anything else. On all kinds of talk shows – which had to stay cheerful no matter what, current affairs being public amusement – leading figures of various stripes sat cosily next to each other on sofas to chat about the possible meanings of Christ's travel plans. Rabbis and prominent atheists, agnostics, henotheists, eternal doubters, the chair of the Muslim Executive (who consistently referred to it as the coming of Isa), Anglicans, representatives of religious women's councils . . . yes, they'd even found a Bridgettine nun willing to leave her enclosure and enter the pernicious world so she could shout her joy in a voice that had withered from long years of cloistered life, gesticulating with fingers that had grown crooked from all that lace-making. Their discussions alternated with jazzed-up versions of hymns. 'Oh sacred head, now wounded', but pushed through the grinder of a beat machine. And after that, *live*, the libertine girls of the pop group Brigitte panting out a song from their debut album, *Jesus Sex Symbol*. In their underwear – black. Two commercial breaks later and the studio guests were already talking about Christ as if He was an old friend, the kid from next door who'd made it as a rock star. And the host's eyes were already gleaming at the thought that he might soon have the Lamb of God Himself on *his* talk show. The ratings would go through the roof!

'*So, Jesus . . . It's all right if I just call you Jesus, isn't it? Yeah? Thanks . . . Could you finally let the cat out of the bag, because this is a question that we, of course, have been dying to ask for a good twenty centuries now . . . Those apostles of yours, they can't have all been straight, surely?*'

These shows were so relaxed and light-hearted, entertaining above all, that we almost forgot to notice that no-one, neither the nihilist nor the Antichrist, questioned the veracity of the newspaper reports. The free-thinkers expressed their enthusiasm, in anticipation of the philosophical riches that an encounter with such a shining light would be sure to generate. The Marxists – who traditionally depicted the Nazarene as a big morphine pump designed to keep the masses in ignorance – praised the anarchistic characteristics of a man who, like Che Guevara, preferred to die for His ideals rather than live a lie, and hoped to soon greet Him as the forefather of leftist philosophy.

For the time being there wasn't a single cry of panic. The Jehovah's Witnesses zipped their lips and didn't say a word about the countdown to the Last Days having begun. As if anyone would have listened anyway, seeing as the world ended every five years or so, according to their calculations. Defeatists and kiss-my-arsists everywhere indulged in childish excitement, the sceptics put the mockers under lock and key – it was a moving sight.

All the more remarkable were the sour faces with which the Catholic authorities endured the debate. If anything, you would have expected the leading figures of this ancient institution to be delirious with joy about the arrival of their Shepherd. And they could definitely have used a religious revival: they celebrated their Sunday Masses for a few drooling bags of bones, the increasing vacancy of their places of worship was constantly obliging the National Trust to rezone a church here and a basilica there as a discotheque or fashion boutique. And that wasn't even the deepest point of the pit they were in. The stench hanging over our bishoprics was billowing up from suppurating wounds that had finally been laid bare.

It wasn't as if the news of a priest having molested a child was such a total shock that the population couldn't get over it. The wandering fingers of priests and brothers featured in too many popular jokes for the actual clergy to have ever been clear of suspicion, because that same populace, proverb mad, has lived for centuries in the wise belief that where there's smoke there must be fire. Everyone was familiar with the twinkle that appears in the youth movement chaplain's eye while inspecting his cub scouts at their washtubs. Every year the boarding schools produced a new generation of boys who had felt a priest's clammy hand on their necks, who knew how a manly voice could tremble during the Hosanna if the singer's eyes were fixed on a troop of boyish faces. On the day of the public announcement of his exam results, many a college student – and what could be more beautiful than a youth proudly venturing into adulthood with his tie twisted and crooked because it's the first time he's tied it himself – thought back on the Jesuit fingers in his mouth as the priest theatrically positioned a host on his tongue. And how that finger always left behind a taste of tobacco. That too would be on the graduates' minds before they threw themselves into the drink and drowned the past; a close-knit teenage clique before they burst apart as lawyers and doctors, members of professions people named with less pride, and failures. Students who had once signed up as altar boys would soon

16

walk through the large gates of the Catholic school for the last time, knowing that the image of the sperm stain on the chasuble would stick with them like a youthful sorrow. The sleeping cubicles had left a mark on their characters – it was there that the night supervisor had groped them in the crotch – but now they were receiving their diplomas and ready for the Great Forgetting.

To a degree, the masses were able to forgive these members of religious orders their scarcely concealed horniness, given the inevitability of slow perversion for those living under the rule of celibacy. Yes, these priests and monks could even count on pity.

But recently a bomb had dropped on the image of the Catholic Church. Yet another. One of the victims of a randy bishop had been smart enough to tape his conversations with the ecclesiastical authorities and these recordings left no room for doubt about how vigorously the Church had tried to manoeuvre the young man into a corner. He, the victim, was the one with a problem, because he – that's right, the victim – was the one who was failing to resolve his problems in a pastoral fashion. Because this wasn't something you needed to hang out in public, it wasn't a matter to be considered by courts of law, incompetent as they were to judge cases that

God was so much cleverer at resolving. It wasn't the rapist who was failing as a Christian, but the raped, because he found it impossible to *forgive* his tormentors. He should be ashamed of himself.

The Church cravenly embraced the role of injured party, even accusing the victim of wanting to profit from the situation by seeking damages. All over the country Masses were dedicated to the paedophile bishop, with prayers to support him through these undoubtedly difficult days. And to spare him the wrath of the mob, he was tucked away in a Trappist monastery, where the beer tasted quite a bit better than the liquids civil perpetrators of sexual offences get to drink in their overcrowded cells. No apologies. The clergy was entirely free of sin, always, and untouchable.

Of course, we'd let ourselves be lulled into a state of drowsiness. This was the same institution that had used the search for the Holy Grail as a cheap excuse to indulge itself in excesses of pure racism. The same institution that derived great sadistic pleasure from the Inquisition, flagrantly raping young girls because virgins weren't allowed to be burnt at the stake, rampaging through villages to rip open corsets and squeeze breasts in search of marks from the Devil's tongue. The same institution that knew before others about the Holocaust, the deportation and gassing of an endless stream of people, mostly Jews, and kept quiet, because it was easier that way. That same institution – because after all these years it really was still the same, that was the only conclusion we could draw – now remained as silent as the grave about all the paedophilia scandals within the Church. The psychological mutilation of children was, and remained, subordinate to the reputation of the Holy Church, amen.

And now Christ was coming to Brussels.

The last time the Mother of God appeared in Brussels was in 1972, to complain to a poor, randomly chosen frump about all the abuses behind the façade of the Catholic Church.

The clergy could put two and two together. They were pissing themselves with terror and there was hardly a dry habit in the house. This time it wasn't the Mother coming their way, but the utmost authority in the whole universe. To call *them* to account – no other reason imaginable! And the bishops looked as pale as all those children when they were panting their cigary breath into their faces.

News has to entertain. And once again it had done an excellent job of just that.

That night I caught myself starting to make the sign of the cross. I mean, the reflex still seemed to be there. An old, ancient habit from my childhood, when my grandparents drew crosses on my forehead with their thumbs when I was going up to bed, something that always made me feel safe. I'd stopped praying long ago. I had simply lost my faith. My horror of death had grown and in exchange I had become proud of the independence of my thought. But now I suddenly felt my right hand rising towards my forehead, a habit I thought I'd shrugged off long ago. I only needed to lose control for a moment and I'd start mumbling, *Oh Lord, ev'ning has now fallen*, begging for His blessing, peace and forgiveness. I would have discovered just how well I had memorised all those prayers and to what degree their mantras could still soothe me. But I managed to pull my hand back just in time and grabbed my wife instead. And that, too, was a form of prayer.

Third Station

The next day, when I went for a walk to pick up the paper – more of a stroll really – I was struck by the sight of an elderly woman who had set up camp alongside the Place des Palais. At that stage there were still more than three weeks left to count down until the arrival of the Most High, but this lady wasn't letting the grass grow under her feet and had already assumed position in a beach chair, armed with an ice box, a small shopping trolley filled with tinned food, and a fairly large portrait of the Lord that seemed to me in danger of succumbing to the first downpour. On a cardboard sign, she'd written '*Lord I am not worthy to have You come to me, yet You have come. Thank You*', with a few endearing spelling and grammatical errors that I, out of piety, have chosen not to reproduce here. And so she sat there, determined not to budge an inch from her chair. Against a backdrop of travel-mad Japanese tourists who gravitated to this neighbourhood, toothless pensioners shuffling to the ducks in the nearby park with bags of saved-up crusts, young lovers who were still satisfied with just a bench and each other, joggers, numerous dog owners who had to leave their gardenless homes several times a day to meet their pets' requirements, crammed sightseeing buses with day-trippers who kept their cameras aimed hopefully at the royal balcony, exhaust fumes . . . To me, the scene seemed more surrealistic than the Magrittes that charmed the dreamers in the art gallery around the corner.

This lady had apparently jumped straight to the conclusion that Christ would be including the royal palace in His visit. And why not? A fellow king, after all. Her presence forced us, and with us the city council, to think about a likely route. For myself, I would have sent the Son of God off on the path of the discontented, the north-south axis over the Boulevards Jacqmain, Anspach and Lemonnier: streets that have often been the conduit for a cacophony of megaphones, horns, rattles and curses. Where the crew of the Iceland trawlers came to scream their dissatisfaction at the new fishing quotas, where Pyrenean sheep shearers begged for a humane price for their wool, where farmers sprayed their liquid manure and emptied their milk churns and the employees of the steelworks roared for a more equitable Europe; here, where people had hoped to march racism right out of the world, where they had believed in the effectiveness of slogans and chanted 'no nukes, no war' in a single voice, where the unions had come from every corner of the old continent to display their abhorrence for the power of money, where effigies had been lit and rotten eggs hurled . . . that was the path, in my mind at least, that Christ should follow in this city. The route of the unhappy masses, the eternal etceteras, the enslaved, the poverty-stricken. But heading to the royal palace was another option too, of course. It just depended on how you wanted to see it.

The old woman's foresight did not go unnoticed. Her move got her onto the local TV station's midday news, and that set the ball rolling. By evening the Place des Palais most resembled a campground, and well-equipped families who weren't planning on missing a single second of the historic event were still flooding into the neighbourhood, despite the official bodies' refusal to confirm that this area had indeed been included on the route.

Seeing this little old lady, one of God's groupies, I inadvertently thought of my own mother. I say inadvertently because, all in all, I think very little about my mother and far less than I might be expected to. But it occurred to me that perhaps she too might like to be present at this unlikely event. If I wasn't mistaken, she had, during a sprightlier phase of her life, witnessed John Paul II kissing the tarmac of the small airport of, I think, Wevelgem. Even if that might have been mainly due to her then employer's devout decision to mark the papal visit by granting paid leave to every baptised employee.

In the meantime, an unaided afternoon in the centre of Brussels had become too difficult for her, given her respectable age, her fear of the metro and her anxiety about bombings and various other things. With me along she might have been braver, and that left me only one option: I had to ask her.

She lived on the Avenue Charles Quint, close to the clunky Koekelberg Basilica, three floors up in the kind of grey apartment you find in large numbers in most cities. The owner refused to rent to coloured tenants – out of principle, because they bred like rats and, when it came down to it, his flats weren't equipped for big raucous families. This meant that the profitability of this slum lord's poorly maintained dumps depended on newly infatuated couples with bottom-of-the-ladder wages and old-age pensioners with no other means of support and a compromised sense of smell, which didn't encourage him to do anything about the stench rising from the rubbish chute either.

My mother's canary was at its most cheerful in the

morning between seven and nine, when the commuters on the road downstairs lost their patience and treated the neighbourhood to a concerto of car horns. It gave the creature something to do, lustily answering all those urban noises. Until the evening rush hour came to relieve its imprisonment again, the bird, Flutter by name, had to entertain itself with the listless swing of the pendulum and four or five weather reports. But from where she read her gossip mags, my mother did have a view of the only cow the city of Brussels had left, a bonus that any real-estate agent worth his salt would advertise in bold letters. Every year when the butchering season was leaving cowsheds all over the country that little bit quieter, people started worrying about the arrival of a developer. Because it was clear that every blade of grass was a barrier to the economy. What was the benefit of letting a cow snort up diesel fumes day in, day out? Her milk could only be a source of lead poisoning! The national interest would be much better served by building an office block! But still, for the time being, the cow was holding firm against all kinds of expansionism – according to rumours, because of the burgeoning strength of the environmentalist lobby – and both the field and the occasional mooing of its grazer granted my mother and others an illusion of nature. When preparing thoroughly urbanised children for their First Holy Communion and searching for a few concrete Bible references, catechists would conveniently ignore the negligible differences between an ox and a cow, and take their students to the small field on the Avenue Charles Quint: standing there before them was a descendant of the privileged beast that was present at the birth of the baby Jesus in Bethlehem; the steam from the nose of this pierced creature had, in the miraculous year zero, drifted over the manger, briefly leaving a pleasant warmth behind. Atheistic parents stressed other points in their educational attempts and could be seen on weekends standing at the barbed wire around this patch of lawn giving a detailed explanation of the miracle known as a cow. Eyes wide, the littlies stared at the animal's dangling bagpipes, struggling to believe that this could be the source of tubs of yoghurt.

Anyway, that was where my mother lived, and she – judging by the volume she invariably set her TV at – had lost most of her hearing.

The lift was working – miracles upon miracles that week.

It occurred to me that I had never before invited my mother on any kind of excursion at all. Other people take their parents out now and then, to a pancake restaurant here, a market or theatre production there. Some of them even take them on holiday with them. Not me. The only outings I went on with my mother were to the Erasmus Hospital, where they occasionally recalculated the use-by date of her artificial hip. From her perspective, the worst thing about visiting the doctor was the taxi ride, as there was a ten-to-one chance of the driver being North African. To celebrate surviving the ride *and* being given a clean bill of health, she would buy us a treat at the hospital cafeteria. A *carré confiture*: braided pastry filled with apricot jam. What you could call a family tradition.

I wasn't altogether sure that my suggestion of going to cheer the Good Shepherd would meet with her approval. Perhaps she wouldn't appreciate being lumped together with the flag-and-banner-waving simpletons along the route. And as far as the depth or otherwise of her faith went, I didn't have a clue. True, she had kept the Bible she'd clasped angelically to please the portrait photographer on the day of her First Holy Communion, but I'd never seen her read a single word of it. A crucifix hung above the kitchen door, a decoration that gives the owner the pleasure of dusting it once a week but is otherwise completely ignored. Two palms were wedged in behind the back of the semi-naked deity, almost like feathers in the arse of a burlesque dancer, and the leaves looked so dried and bleached that it could only mean that it had been decades since my mother had last attended Mass on Palm Sunday. She ignored religious obligations like Ash

27

Wednesday and her insatiable hunger for chocolates was a hurdle to any interest she might have had in Lent. She had sent me to a Catholic school, but only because she assumed they would give me a better education, a belief she shared with many others of her generation. The cold church benches put a chill in my mother's waterworks during weddings and funerals only, the latter significantly more frequent than the former. If Christian groups appeared on her doorstep begging for donations to set up a school in Port-au-Prince or sink a well in a parched part of Africa, she slammed the door in their faces. So no, I couldn't be sure that her heart was imbued with Christ's teachings. What's more, she was a sinner in the clerical sense of the word: an unmarried mother who had refused to confess the name of the father, even to the child.

'Look who's shown up, my prodigal son! Would you like something to drink?'

There are actually only two beverages I really like: beer and coffee. It was too early for beer, I thought. And since stinginess had tightened its already firm grip on her, my mother had taken to reusing her coffee filters several times. Once she started doing that, I knew she had grown old. Her taste buds were completely shot – fortunately for her. The sight of her going crazy with the pepper grinder over a bowl of soup left no room for doubt. But I wouldn't derive any pleasure from the vague recollection of coffee provided by her watery infusions of infusions.

'I'm fine, thanks.'

'Hasn't Claudia come with you?'

'Veronique!'

'What?'

'Veronique! It's been almost fifteen years since I was with Claudia. It's Veronique, Mum, can't you remember that?'

'It doesn't matter anyway. You've come by yourself, that says enough.'

While speaking to me, she kept her face turned to the TV. I joined her in watching a cook pretentiously arrange three leaves of crinkly lettuce on a plate, undoubtedly in the hope that this would make the lettuce taste a little less like lettuce.

'Do you want something to drink?'

'You just asked me that, Mum!'

'Did I? What did you say?'

'That I was fine, thanks.'

The cook disappeared from the TV screen, replaced by a vet.

It was time for me to come up with my suggestion. Cautiously, scared as I was of making myself look ridiculous. The point was, in our house, religion had always been on a par with sexuality in the sense that it was something private, not really taboo, but private. You didn't talk about it, end of story.

'Have you heard that Jesus is coming to Brussels?'

'That's all they talk about.'

'Would it be interesting to be there when he goes through the streets?'

Finally she took her eyes off the stupid, mind-numbing TV. She looked straight at me as if trying to decide what to do: laugh out loud or give me an earful.

She dangled her false teeth in the middle of her mouth, a tic she always had when weighing her words, and finally said, 'All those people standing on the side of the road three weeks in advance aren't very sure of themselves. People who believe they'll have plenty of opportunity to see God don't need to go to all kinds of lengths to catch a quick glimpse of Him during their earthly existence.'

Needless to say, her answer surprised me. I had anticipated all kinds of things, but never such a sharp analysis. When, just a few hours after this declaration, my mother died unexpectedly in her sleep with a blissful smile on her face the like of which the coffin maker had never seen on a client before, my astonishment was complete.

And so it was that in a period I should remember as one of the most beautiful in my already fairly advanced life, I found myself lowering my mother's body into the soil of Evere Cemetery.

At Dupont, the nearby café where mourners often go to console themselves with rabbit stew and a Trappist beer, I ate a *carré confiture* and felt, appropriately or not, inexplicably happy. In the days ahead I had to clear out an apartment in which I might find a photo of the man who could be my father, a letter too perhaps, and I would liberate a canary from its horrible cage.

Fourth Station

Since 1698 Brussels has had its very own way of declaring its love for someone – namely, dressing the city's best-known statue up as the object of veneration. Manneken Pis – and what other statue could I be talking about? – has already let his pee splash into the fountain on the Rue de l'Étuve decked out as Elvis Presley and Nelson Mandela. As Baden Powell, Mozart, Columbus, a footballer from Racing Anderlecht, a wearer of the Tour de France yellow jersey, as Saint Nicholas, you name it . . . The curly-headed urchin has offended public decorum by day and by night in so many guises. Anyone who has seen this bronze softy demonstrating his perfectly groomed prostate in his capacity as French crooner Maurice Chevalier will find it impossible to listen to 'I Wonder Where My Baby Is Tonight' again without thinking of a willy so puny it couldn't offend a withered old nun.

Paris has the Eiffel Tower; Rome, the Trevi Fountain. For

a long time it bothered me that we were stuck with a nude pisser as our national symbol, as if we were trying to hide our lack of ambition behind cheap bums-and-tits humour. I was equally incapable of understanding why tours from all corners of the globe led to this statue, just fifty-eight centimetres tall, something you'd walk past at a flea market without batting an eyelid.

But I became cheerful, very cheerful, when I suddenly saw our Manneken dressed up as Christ with a halo on his head, fishing his widdler up out of his loincloth and peeing, peeing constantly with one hand on his hip and his knees bent slightly to admire what his tummy would otherwise conceal. The penny dropped and I realised that there was no better way of symbolising a sense of liberation than with this statue of a pisser. A male pisser, a young pisser, because he hasn't lost the habit of making sure that his jet arches up so that it can surrender to gravity properly, knowing that its ballistic glory will be cherished. All at once I found this unsightly icon of my equally unsightly country much more triumphant than all the heroes hacked out of marble in the centre of Florence. Triumphant and full of joie de vivre. And I counted my blessings at living in a place where no wars were going to break out because our primary prophet, from a cultural-historical point of view, had been depicted with his pee-pee showing. No outraged preachers screaming blue murder and demanding the reintroduction of the fig leaf in the visual arts. Our Lord's pecker did not shock us. If Giovanni Bellini could already entrust Jesus's minuscule kiddy's dick to canvas in the Early Renaissance – as if the painter wanted to emphasise God's becoming human by endowing him so poorly in the one area where every man, and every woman too actually, is always happy to see a few grams extra – why should we kick up a fuss so many centuries later about a Jesus who didn't feel obliged to hide a single centimetre of Creation?

And, in keeping with Brussels city council policy for all highly exceptional occasions, now too the fountain's pipes were connected to a keg of beer. Until the day of Christ's arrival, Manneken Pis would swathe himself in a halo and loincloth and colour the basin in the Rue de l'Étuve amber.

Speaking for my own generation – the children of the sixties, years that are invariably commemorated on record covers with golden adjectives – I can only say that hope drove us to the point of delirium at the sight of this Manneken Pis. It was forgivable. We had been hurled into the world just when it seemed ready to take revenge on the past. Evil had been purged from mankind with plastic, bubble gum and rock 'n' roll. That was why Germany got to organise the Olympic Games again in '72, to wash away all memories of the propagandist edition of 1936. With renewed naivety – and unfortunately that's the right word, as much as I would like to see things differently – mankind raised its morale with the belief that sport could bring nations closer together and that the path to freedom ran over a 400-metre track. But no matter how much hockey people played or how they excelled in badminton, no matter how fast they swam or how high they jumped, the dream of brotherhood burst when Palestinian terrorists caused a bloodbath and sent the Israeli team home with more coffins than medals. We became acquainted with a new reality of terrorist attacks; police stations swapped their ticket books for PSG1 sniper rifles. In our childhood memories, we eat sausages and sprouts with nutmeg in front of the TV: car bombs and hijacked planes are the newsreader's subjects and our meal tastes none the worse for it. Death tolls roll past like lotto numbers, hostage dramas are our daily fare. Military superpowers threaten to top each other with their all-obliterating nuclear arsenals. And the emaciated Biafran with his gut full of extra-cellular fluid rattles his mess tin as if to say, 'Here I am again, your quiz show's about to start. Thanks for watching, see you tomorrow!'

Industry turned against its manpower, the ranks of the unemployed swelled, the prosperous Valhalla our parents had lit up with jukebox lights had disappeared. We were confronted by new preachers and followers of the racism that had caused so much damage forty years earlier that Europe still hadn't recovered. Gruff and numb and dumb, we resigned ourselves to the role that the end of the filthiest century seemed to be imposing on us.

I was a young man, in the years of my first shaving brush, when my faith in the species unexpectedly revived. Sure, you can put it down to my youthful and defective comprehension of mankind, but still, when the apartheid system collapsed in South Africa, the Cold War was scrapped from the script of the Apocalypse, the Berlin Wall was demolished, velvet revolutions gave the people a voice . . . what was left of my inner utopian rose up and caught the scent of complete vindication at very close quarters. Ideologically, these were my glory days – I'm not ashamed to admit it and I genuinely believe that I'm also speaking for many of my contemporaries. People who had come across as totally apathetic all through university suddenly started wearing Amnesty International T-shirts – without the slightest hint of irony. It was like we were being softened up first to increase the impact of the next blow. Because shortly afterwards, Rwanda demonstrated that genocide only needs 100 days and a few machetes to make the electoral roll a million names lighter. And despite the solemn promise chiselled into so many statues and columns erected after the end of World War II, Srebrenica proved that mass deportations and executions of poor wretches because of their religion, origin or colour were still the order of the day. And the rest of the globe still couldn't give a monkey's! That was the deathblow for my, for our optimistic humanism. We became the famous lost generation, burying itself in middle-class comforts – egotistical, uninspired. The political parties were only too happy to recruit their leaders from our embittered ranks, nobody was interested in the future.

Did we bask in our misery? Absolutely! But out of nowhere a light appeared in our lacklustre days. We felt liberated from the triviality of our banal existences. Or let me just speak for myself, that would be far more honest: I felt liberated from the triviality of my banal existence. And that feeling, which I became more and more conscious of as I stood there in the Rue de l'Étuve, was so striking and – frankly – moving, that I did something I had never thought possible: I walked into a souvenir shop and bought myself a Manneken Pis replica. Thirty euros for a plastic knockoff. The shop assistant was baffled: normally she only ever sold them to tourists; today it had been almost all locals.

Fifth Station

In Belgium it's easier to find a parliamentarian than someone who can sharpen your tools for you. Our country boasts no less than six parliaments – at least when all of our chosen representatives are capable of forming a government simultaneously. A federal government, a Walloon regional government, a Flemish government, a government for the Brussels-Capital region, a government of the French community and a government of the German-speaking community. That's quite something. Six – I repeat, six! – different governments for a nation that occupies at most 30,000 km^2 – smaller than Bhutan, smaller than Guinea-Bissau – ensuring 537 parliamentary pay packets each month. And on top of that, 48 ministers and 10 state secretaries pocket fat salaries, money that could have been used for something else. Some ministers job-hop from one government to another during a single term, which doesn't simplify the wage calculations. Suffice to say that the structure of our state institutions is a favourite subject for examiners with sadistic tendencies, and few words appear as frequently in our editorials as 'Kafkaesque'.

On travels abroad in recent years I'd noticed having to explain more and more often that we weren't in the throes of civil war. The discrepancy between the political discourse and civil life could hardly have been more glaring. Flemings and Walloons weren't at each other's throats: our bricklayers worked together on the same building sites, and the walls they built stood straight and true; the orchestra of La Monnaie was made up of musicians from north and south, but they still managed to play *La Finta Giardiniera* in the same key; people married across the language borders and started households in which the doors slammed and the pots banged neither more nor less often than in other homes, they found the same warmth, the same chill in each other's arms. But still our biggest loudmouths shouted the populist slogans that gave outsiders the opposite impression and scared off crucial investors.

Be that as it may, it was time to start thinking about an official delegation, bigwigs who would share the stage with Christ and press His flesh for the photographers who would undoubtedly turn out in large numbers for the occasion. It was the Flemish ministers who pounded the table first, to no-one's surprise. First and hardest. Brussels was *their* capital, *basta*. After all, the Walloon prime minister resided in the Elysette of Namur where, when the wind was right, he could hear the wild boars grunting in the nearby woods. The Flemish Parliament, on the other hand, was located in the capital on the Boulevard du Roi Albert II, where modern-day Mary Magdalenes climbed into dark cars of an evening. Further-more, and for the northerners this was totally decisive, the Flemish people were closer to God than the Walloons! Their commitment to God and Flanders had always been absolute. More than a century ago, in the days when the spelling was progressive if nothing else, they had summarised their total dedication to Flanders and Christ with the slogan '*Alles Voor Vlaanderen, Vlaanderen Voor Kristus*', a credo that was perfectly suited to arch mispronunciation when being sung during parades and that, as AVVVVK, provided work in flag makers' studios for many a letter embroiderer. Every year, four or so coaches full of rabid advocates of Flemish independence, accompanied by two priests and a thurible of incense and gripped by the notion that the Creator looked favourably on their separatist ideals, headed off to the polder to pray in the open, well-fertilised air, then do their best to evoke the senti-ments of an oppressed minority. Drum rolls and flag-waving were useful aids. When, elsewhere on their calendar, their delight regarding their cultural identity had swollen to such proportions that they had to sing it out, they would gather in the Antwerp sports hall to roar 'On the Purple Heath', 'Lights Shining on the Scheldt' and 'Mieke Grab the Branches of the Trees', interspersed – it's true – with other, more profane sing-along material. Wallonia, on the other hand, had fumigated its faith with industrial smog, the pealing of its church bells had been dulled by the sulphurous haze. The point being: 'Walloons have no business trying to come before Christ at all and definitely not in Brussels!'

Still, if you went looking for a book shop in the shade of the Atomium, you'd find a lot more *librairies* than *boekhandels*, and in the bedrooms people made *l'amour* considerably more often than *de liefde*. You would, in other words, have to spend a long time searching the area around Central Station before finding someone who yodelled 'Lights Shining on the Scheldt' while lathering his perm under the shower. Of all the brides-to-be getting a quick hymen reconstruction on the sly in Brussels hospitals, there were very few who were able to hum the tune of 'Our Lady of Flanders'. Let alone sing it in Dutch.

(. . . 'Our Lady of Flanders': the magnum opus of composer Lodewijk de Vocht. One couldn't help but wonder in which prefab neighbourhood, in which car park of which horticultural supplies depot the man's statue stood . . . And how many pigeons had already shat it to the point of unrecognisability . . .)

But that a *true* delegation of the city and nation would include French speakers was beyond question.

And that forgotten percentile of German-speaking Belgians – always quiet, withdrawn and unassuming in their grassy corner, denizens of no-man's land who understood that life, essentially, is all about filling milk churns – suddenly they too spoke up loud and clear to demand a role in the ceremonial proceedings related to the reception of Our Lord.

And so our policy-makers slipped back into the time-honoured practice of inter-community squabbling, the thing they loved to hide behind to avoid having to discuss the potholes in our roads, the affordability of our educations, the pollutants in our soil and the decrepitude of our nuclear reactors.

It wasn't just the nation – the capital too was crumbled up into a confusing plethora of executive levels. No less than nineteen bellies in this one city were wrapped with a mayoral sash. Brussels was a patchwork quilt of different municipalities, each with a vision that wasn't allowed to extend beyond its own kerb. Until now. Because all at once the mayor of Uccle felt like a purebred *Bruxellois*, even though he didn't have to promise anyone who lived there anything to strengthen his electoral basis. And he insisted on a VIP badge and a seat at Christ's right hand on the big day, which might perhaps be the Day of Judgment itself.

When you consider that the MEPs were also claiming the right to a personal consultation with Jesus, it's easy to understand the despondency surrounding the organisation of the event.

It was hardly surprising: everyone of any name or fame was dying to be photographed next to a man who shared his DNA with God Almighty. Any deeds of nobility that could be conjured up were worthwhile; there was no arse so filthy it wasn't worth kissing; no pride too small or too big that it couldn't be pushed aside to clear the way for some craven toadying. It would be going too far to sum up all of the initiatives taken by shameless individuals, but if one case can serve as an example of all the ridiculous goings-on, then let it be known far and wide that the president of FC Brussels changed the date of the friendly against Standard de Liège's reserve team to the twenty-first of July in the hope that no-one less that the Son of God would take the honorary kick-off.

★

For once, the leaders of the permanent provisional federal government were called back from foreign holiday resorts not to allay a crisis, but to arrange a happy event. They put together a special commission, and to everyone's amazement they did it so quickly that the television producers' hopes of an animated debate were nipped in the bud.

The Val-Duchesse priory had proved itself many times before as an appropriate location for momentous negotiations. It was there that they philosophised their way through every last article of the Treaty of Rome in 1957, adding the finishing touch to what would later become the European Union. Ailing governments went there to break their fall; agreements that had been considered impossible were reached. According to initiates, it was because of the fireplace with its inspirational crackling. Others put it down to the park, where brains could suck up a dose of oxygen before making a difficult decision. And it was also due, undeniably, to the estate's kitchen. *Duo de langoustine et homard en carpaccio à la citronnelle; Limande aux petits gris de Namur, fin bouillon aux lentins de chêne et à la ciboulette chinoise; Saint-Jacques poêlées aux lentilles vertes du Puy, roulade de concombre aux huïtres plates de Colchester, Poule faine à la fine champagne et sa garniture hivernale* . . . You can't make peace when people are hungry. The most pig-headed of

Flemish radicals would drop all linguistic demands at the sight of this menu, opening his mouth wide while already undoing the top button of his trousers as a precautionary measure. As a result, there wasn't a single commission member who showed any signs of sorrow about having to withdraw into gastronomic isolation for the duration of the negotiations.

One discussion point could in any case be laid to rest quickly: anyone who had the ambition of chaperoning Our Saviour during His stay in the city would need to speak His language!

There were still some people who listed a proficiency in Latin on their curriculum vitae. It wasn't a language you could buy a loaf of bread in any more, and even the best-educated girls had long accepted the attentions of boys who kept their ablatives under wraps. But there were a few who had kept their mental muscles limber by studying it during their grammar school years, a cerebral workout that others got by reaching for a chessboard. A more vulgar motive for choosing the subject was to acquire the status that a know-ledge of the pluperfect had long provided in the shadow of the steeple. But this – alas, alack – was only Latin, the language botanists use in private to discuss their dried autumn leaves.

But Christ had multiplied His loaves in *Aramaic*! Ha! He had abused the merchants and moneychangers something rotten in Aramaic. That was the language in which he gave Caiaphas short shrift; in which He helped Lazarus over his paralysis; the language in which, on the Mount of Olives, he prayed his most wrenching prayers; the language in which He, some people dared to suggest, dreamt of the lover He never had.

The members of the committee were just tucking into the *mousse au chocolat* (Was that a subtle hint of cognac?) and looked at each other. Aramaic? Anyone? That would have been nothing short of astonishing. Apart from a few crusty biblical scrolls, Aramaic had been virtually wiped off the face of the planet. Neo-Aramaic, or a comical dialect derived from it, was still spoken by a few people here and there. Assyrian Christians in Iran and Iraq, for instance – there were a few thousand of them left, they'd have to maybe be capable of interpreting a conversation with The Prophet. But going to look for them didn't even bear thinking about, with the poor bastards hiding in the mountains in fear of their lives, the umpteenth diaspora trekking over the globe.

And so it came to pass that the nation's hope and eyes turned to Transit Centre 127. There, in the transit zone of the national airport, behind barbed wire, were those who had exhausted all legal avenues, the undocumented, those who had sought

46

understanding and asylum in vain, waiting for a plane to repatriate them to the one place where they were even less welcome. Given that it hadn't fallen into their laps, it was up to them to pursue happiness across many national borders . . . It was too bad we didn't have any coalmines left, otherwise we could have shoved them in there. Then we would have got some profit out of the happiness they found. Our country was full, crammed full . . . with Ikea, Tonton Tapis and Lederland retail chains. So tell us: where were we supposed to accommodate the poor devils? In the display rooms of all those chains, perhaps? Seeing as all their appeals for refugee status had been denied, these people were illegal. As if they were the personification of a bag of cocaine or a box of explosives. Illegal: imagine hearing it about yourself! That your existence is unauthorised! That your birth was non-statutory! That you weren't actually allowed to exist! They didn't dare to ask more of life than standing underpaid and without a word of thanks at the sink of some restaurant somewhere. They were willing to live in rooms where the mould was so thick on the walls that even the most noxious of gas heaters couldn't make a dent in it. But even that comfort was denied them. They had to go. Back to where their mothers had dropped them. It was the most narrow-minded idea the modern age had brought forth: that the information in your passport defined you!

Mankind had ringed the birds and branded the cows. The last thing it had to squeeze into a catalogue was itself. The species' faith in its own ability to think and act was clearly so lamentably weak that the idea of someone transcending their native soil was considered an impossibility.

There, where the bars crossed out the view, in that heavy-hearted Transit Centre 127, there had to be someone perhaps, among the spurned, whose mother tongue allowed them to make head or tail of old Aramaic. If that could only be true, we'd have an interpreter for Our Lord and that man or woman would immediately receive a definitive resident's permit. Foreign Affairs were already on their way with the stamps.

Sixth Station

I think I had always found Brussels at its most beautiful in the second week of July, when the high ozone concentrations obliged chemists to stock up on asthma inhalers and discount-obsessed women had saddled up for the start of the bargain-hunting season in the Rue Neuve. When the summer holiday casuals were realising that operating a checkout wasn't quite as easy as it had always looked, the civil servants' compasses were turned to the lazy south and for once the city had briefly shrugged off its frantic tides of traffic. A morning in the inhabited world couldn't dawn more beautifully than the one on which the first side-show operators drove their heavily laden trucks through the centre of town. It was time for the summer fair. No sooner had the first lantern been screwed into its fitting than I could already smell the donuts, the waffles, the fritters. And as if it was being poured out over us from the skies, I always heard the stirring voice of Jacques Brel to accompany it, singing: *J'aime la foire où pour trois sous l'on peut se faire tourner la tête.* I can't deny it, summer after summer I was thrilled to watch the hustle and bustle as they filled the entire kilometre between the Porte de Hal and the Porte d'Anderlecht with ice palaces and carousels. Bizarre really, because I wasn't one for crowds. Never had been. But a fair, hothouse for misanthropy that it is, yes . . . There I found the courage to let my mistrust of the mob slide. It wasn't something I could explain either.

It's been a long time since three sous was enough to get yourself swung upside down through the domain of the birds. Far from it: most fairground rides now offer the ultimate entertainment of a near-death experience at a price that puts a serious dent in the average family budget. But the dodgems had fortunately survived many a fashion and still provided youths with an ideal and affordable backdrop for puffing up their chests, throwing their shoulders back, coolly smoking cigarettes and ogling the opposite sex, the last-mentioned with undoubtedly more courage and self-confidence than I had at their age. It was one of the few things I treated myself to every fair: the dodgems, three or four rides. Of course, I wasn't a threat to any of the youthful machos and nobody got any fun out of ramming me in the side. They tolerated me in their territory as an aged and increasingly pathetic relic, freewheeling through his frayed and threadbare nostalgia. The only contemporaries I encountered under the neon lights were men who had splashed down into fatherhood fairly late in life and were giving their son, or occasionally their daughter, a playful initiation into the art of driving. Having already had some dealings with osteopaths, they knew what whiplash was and took the name dodgem literally, no longer seeing the cars as vehicles for ramming each other, but regarding them purely as didactic devices for teaching their progeny the rules of the road. So yes, I couldn't really argue with the youths who saw me as a lost and pitiable melancholic when I steered my car over the battleground, their battleground. All the same, I couldn't break the habit of always climbing back into a dodgem. Now too, as the steel skeletons of all kinds of gigantic whirling machines were being screwed together, I realised that I would grip the steering wheel again this year, and felt a remnant of the old excitement that had thrown my nervous system into an uproar so many years ago, women ago, sorrows ago, when the arrival of the fair rang like a promise.

This neighbourhood could do with a little enchantment, and that's another reason I had always looked forward to the arrival of the showmen. These stubborn romantics liberated us from ugliness, and as liberators they deserved to be greeted like the chain-smoking Canadians on the Avenue de Tervueren on the third of September, 1944. If this required our girls to accept the responsibility that came with their charms, so be it: *Deus vult!*

I am exaggerating . . . slightly. But there's no denying that the Boulevard Poincaré had been growing greyer for years. Of all the things we have had to accept in this neighbourhood, few went down as easily as the deceits of a Ferris wheel by night, a mechanical supernova lifting us up above our daily shades of grey. During these luminous weeks, faces were glued to the windows of the international trains pulling out of South Station, and their fixed expressions betrayed their regret that an ultra-fast railway line had been drilled through the bed of the Channel. They would have rather stayed a little longer, now that the temperatures made it even more enjoyable to knock back a cold *gueuze* and the time had come for Belgians to exhaust themselves discussing the merits of the new season's mussels. But the demands our era placed on train traffic were unrelenting, only two croissants separated the Grand Place from Piccadilly Circus. And as time and money are two maggots that feed on the same corpse, there were share hunters who were convinced that the travelling time between Brussels and London could and should be reduced to just one croissant. By the time Jacques Brel launched into the next verse, the commuters of commerce were already deeper than the cod

Et nous donnant un peu de rêve pour que les hommes soient contents.

Each time the neighbourhood took on the promising aroma of horse shit, deposited from the well-styled rear ends of jaded fairground ponies, I readied myself for a walk past the attractions – a walk which took me, at the same time, past the past itself. I found the sentimentality cloying, but what could I do? Each visit to the fair was a visit to the fairgrounds of yesteryear. I immersed myself in the calls of ticket-selling stallholders and searched for the spider lady, the travelling cabinet of Siamese twins, the caterpillar. Languidly, I wandered through memories of the brasserie Caulier-Express Midi – where I once drank my first beer and pretended to like the taste – of boxers and wrestlers, of teenage infatuations that blossomed and shrivelled during one and the same summer.

But still something seemed different this time. Something essential. Of course, various machines catapulted the avidly screeching girls up into thin air higher and faster than they had the year before, and a ride on the carousel was a lot dearer than it had been 360 days earlier. But that wasn't essential.

What I'm trying to say is that this fair suddenly had more to do with the future than with the past. This time the fair deserved its place; it was justified now, simply because there was something to celebrate.

Were my eyes deceiving me, or were the immigrant families loading up their vans with reluctance, preparing for a reunion with their more and more estranged kin in Morocco, a left-behind grandmother whose peace of mind required them to keep quiet about how difficult it was to survive in Europe? And was I seeing things, or were there residents who had suddenly put out window boxes here and there? Residents who had *dared* to put out window boxes? Because you can be sure that anyone who had ever taken the trouble of adding a little colour and life to decorate the façade of their home and, with it, the neighbourhood had quickly relented. A significant number of the city's many unemployed youths were convinced that, along with the window boxes and bus stops, they were demolishing their own boredom. A few brave souls persisted in their civic contribution to beautification by arming themselves with a brush and pan and immediately replacing the window box, but I've never had the privilege of meeting someone with enough determination or naivety to put out a third. As a consequence, we should be grateful for the existence of satellite dishes, otherwise many of our façades would look even more cheerless. But now one window box after another was appearing in the streetscape; you couldn't believe your eyes.

Beleaguered travel agencies came up with more and more aggressive advertising, splashing out with discounts, free this and even freer that, in an attempt to jumpstart the hitherto disappointing bookings for July, which was, after all, the make-or-break month for their annual turnover. ('Jumpstart': a buzzword used by sad cases who drag themselves from one conference to the next.) Inversely, the price of a Brussels hotel room, with or without stars, shot up to dizzying heights. The celery in the allotments near Laerbeek Wood had to make way for an improvised campground, and anyone who was short on conscience and hoped to turn a profit from the special situation rented out their utility room as a bed and breakfast for the ever-increasing stream of pilgrims.

And it was true really. If our city was, briefly, the navel of the world, why should we spend our holidays elsewhere?

By chance, and unusually for us, Veronique and I hadn't yet planned a trip for that summer. Perhaps we'd been afraid, each of us separately, that we wouldn't survive a holiday as a couple – that was how deep a rut our relationship had been in for the last year. We were tired of each other. I had started to calculate how much of myself I had given up to be absorbed in this unity of two. It would be too coarse to claim that it was only convenience that was keeping us together, but an undeniable curiosity about other ways of life had crept into my thoughts, an interest in the greener grass on the other side of the fence. You didn't need to be a psychologist to know that the chance of falling ecstatically in love with the first stranger to come along was greater than ever. That applied to her, it applied to me.

Was that what I wanted?

Sometimes! But, and this was important too, not always!

'You're too private, but it's not your fault,' she had once said, and she wasn't the first of my partners to raise this theory. 'You never had a father. You were always alone with your mother . . . There was no-one to teach you how to live together.'

Veronique's holidays had started too now. Three weeks without deadlines, crammed inboxes or ringing telephones. By the time she'd more or less relaxed into a life away from the grind, it would be time for her to creep back in between her office partitions.

To celebrate the start of our holiday, we slid our legs in under a table at Le Tournant, ordered Italian bubbly and pretended to study the menu, already knowing far in advance

that we would both take the sweetbread. With almond flakes
– you could do worse. Our lack of a travel destination would
come up and I was on edge about that. I knew how much she
suffered from the realisation that a human life was not long
enough to have admired all of the earth's crust, or even a
quarter of it. She was convinced there were deserts out there
just waiting for her. There were mountain passes she needed
to walk through, forests to smell, squirrel monkeys longing
to be patted. For myself, I'd already made up my mind: I
wanted to stay in Brussels this summer, now that the city
had rediscovered its faith in itself and was undergoing a
completely unexpected renaissance, with metro tunnels that,
at first sniff, smelt a fraction less like piss and were being
livened up by local oom-pa-pa music by Grand Jojo, Coco
Van Babbelgem and other half-forgotten folk bards. But I
wasn't anticipating a round of applause after announcing my
personal holiday plans. Inasmuch as I'd lost my calling as a
fortune teller, I expected Veronique to respond by going travelling without me. Broad-minded couples wouldn't make a
problem of something like that, marriage is not a prison; after
all, you mustn't restrict each other's individual freedom. But
I was level-headed enough to know what that freedom came
down to in the end.

'We still haven't booked anything for the summer . . .'

She hadn't sounded indignant or disillusioned. She had

just presented it as a matter-of-fact observation. We hadn't booked anything yet, full stop.

'No, that's right. Did you have a destination in mind, maybe?'

'Well, there's still plenty of places to see of course. We'll never tick them all off.'

'True.'

'What about you?'

'I don't know. I thought maybe . . .'

'. . . that you'd like to stay home one year for a change?'

'Well . . . You know . . . I still need to clear out my mother's apartment. Until it's completely empty, I have to keep paying the rent. That's one thing. And second, right now Brussels feels so, I don't know, enjoyable. It seems a shame to swap it for a beach or whatever. How can I put it . . . the fair . . . this whole Jesus business . . .'

And her expression seemed to lighten. She'd been thinking exactly the same thing, but hadn't dared say so.

Sometimes predictability has its enjoyable side too: once again the sweetbread was succulent.

On our way home at least forty people spontaneously wished us a pleasant evening.

Seventh Station

She usually dreamt her dreams on worse mattresses. That
was when she was lucky enough to have a mattress at all.
Newspapers spread out on the floor, park benches, flattened
cardboard boxes in deserted shopping arcades – they were the
surfaces on which she generally fell asleep. Compared to that,
the beds in the Transit Centre had been pure luxury. But now,
on one of those mild July nights, eleven-year-old Ohanna
and her parents were suddenly sleeping in the Boulevard
Adolphe Max – the street where wankers young and old try
to wear themselves out in sex-shop peep booths – in the most
expensive beds this city has to offer. The presidential suite of
a hotel. 7,800 euros a night or, according to the statistics of the
moment, five times the average monthly wage. Magnates,
ministers and oil sheiks had slept between these very same
sheets.

The suite measured three hundred and forty square metres

and the hotel's interior decorators had reduced the awkward, empty feeling by decking it out with disproportionately enormous TV screens and, almost inevitably, a Jacuzzi. If guests found its ugliness too much to bear, they could camouflage most of it reasonably well with the lighting – computer controlled, of course. Standing discreetly in the background was a butler with a postgraduate degree in the silent removal of champagne corks and an exceptionally well-feathered nest, thanks to the tips slipped him by numerous lonely women. A chauffeur-driven Jaguar was available for guests who wished to venture out into the world they could see though the triple-glazed windows and – because you can work up a sweat living even the cushiest of lives – there was a multi-jet shower for them to wash themselves in.

Foreign Affairs had selected Ohanna to accompany Christ during His earthly sojourn. Officially because, considering her origins and innate linguistic sensitivity, there was a high probability of her grammar closely approaching the original Aramaic. Her being chosen ahead of, amongst others, the eager Jewish applicants for the honour may have been closely related to her age. Still a child in all things.

'Suffer the little children to come unto Me.' It was a sentence that more than one ministry staffer remembered as having been spoken by the Lord, or rather, thought they could remember, because attempts to find that particular quote in the Bible were thwarted by the arrival of the coffee break. But choosing a child was usually a safe bet, just ask the ad men. Kids could be an enormous pain in the neck, but once you put that detail out of your mind, it was easy to accept a child as a symbol of absolute innocence. What's more, Ohanna had a cute little face that could have been plucked straight from a UNICEF calendar – the month of May, for instance. There was no better way of showing Christ the concern people in Belgium felt for the powerless and the outsiders, knowing that as a child He too had been a power-less outsider, so much so that His Mother had been forced to secretly drop Him in a stable, out of sight and smelling range, as if He were a piece of shit she couldn't keep in a moment longer.

Her selection gave Ohanna and her parents a future – that was a miracle in itself and something they'd no longer dared hope for – but the great responsibility that had been thrust upon her weighed heavily on her delicate shoulders. She had to do the job with verve, otherwise she and the rest of her family would be flown straight back to misery. No wonder the task preyed on her mind day and night: she thought about it when she got up in the morning and in the evening when she went to bed, and even when she was asleep her dreams brought it back. Her parents were counting on her. The country was counting on her, the European Union, the Vatican perhaps. What choice did she have? She had to do her work perfectly, and that meant showing the Son of God Brussels as it really was, the city she knew all too well, a place where a quarter of the population didn't have a pot to piss in, where a third of the children, that's right, a third, grew up in families without an income acquired by work. Where one in four sick people postponed medical treatment because dying was more affordable than a cure. She had to show Him the city on a morning when its desperate young were out looking for work, with way too many of them thronging together at the windows of the employment agencies, battling for the same dirty jobs in the full knowledge that thirty per cent of them would never see a payslip. Ever. She had to show Him the schools the young had left prematurely and without a diploma, as sceptical as they were about the value of one of those signed scraps of paper, if only because their fathers – despite banging on constantly about how important they were – had never got anywhere with their own.

★

Ohanna was in luck: in her dream she was standing on a grey platform at North Station, in the middle of a neighbourhood she knew well. Jesus stepped out of a graffiti-covered carriage, second class, as could be expected, and into the fried-onion smell of a nearby black pudding stall. She spotted Him at once and said: 'Welcome, Jesus Christ, Messiah and only-begotten Son of God, to Brussels, the capital of the Kingdom of Belgium, the capital of the Flemish and French-speaking communities, the administrative centre of the European Union and home to NATO. We are most honoured by Your coming.' Exactly as she had been taught. Then she took Him by the hand, with His permission, and together they took the escalator down to the train station's depressing central concourse with the refreshment bar where surreptitious drunks stopped in the morning to drown their craving for alcohol by slobbering down a few hasty cans of beer before disappearing in front of computers all day, after which they repeated the ritual in the evening until they had poured themselves enough courage to start a stupefying train journey home to prolong their somnambulant marriages. A little further along, numbers and letters rattled into position on the sign that indicated destinations and departure times. No, it's not true, that numerical dance stopped rattling when they started using LED letters to list the latest delays. But in the heads of impatient travellers, the boards still rattle and clack like they did in the days the first locomotive blew out its first furious head of steam. It was lunchtime: at the food stalls, plastic bottles ejaculated threads of mayonnaise into bread rolls filled with ham and cheese for the restless souls who ate their meals on the hoof. Their diaries barked out orders – forward march, left, right, left, right, left, right, left – so loudly, they didn't notice Christ getting in the way.

It was winter in Ohanna's dream; that helped, because she was able to show Him how the station filled with beggars, sluggish from the cold and the diet they scraped together from rubbish-bin specials. Roma Gypsies, wrapped in tattered blankets and misled by their enthusiasm for a destination that had been sold to them as a decent place to live. Vagrants, stubborn drunks, ghosts really, because administratively they were long dead and rotten, stinking from all their encrustations. She introduced Him to Mariëtte, the station's toilet attendant, who was kind enough to allow the homeless free use of her two profitable toilets. And He promptly decorated Mariëtte with His blessing.

Ohanna gripped Jesus's hand even tighter and led Him through the thoughts of the many passers-by – it was a dream, anything was possible, she had to seize the opportunity! And there they saw the conviction that none of these scabby derelicts actually needed alms. How could they? This was a country with all essential social services, there was help for anyone who wanted it; these losers slept on the streets of their own free will. It was true that the babies in the arms of the wretched-looking mothers were real babies that evoked the pity of women who had to dump their own offspring in a crèche during office hours, but they had been rented by the hour from a criminal agency that had discovered how much more appealingly a beggar's cup rattled in a mother's hand. They strolled past the belief that these tramps were dropped off at their begging pitches in the morning by a taxi, a black Mercedes, and that the same vehicle picked them up again in the evening. They were part of well-organised and extremely lucrative companies, purveyors of squalor, and any taxpayer who was prepared to shed one more drop of sweat for an employer needed their head read when you realised the kind of fortunes people accumulated just sitting on their bum on the floor of a train station.

Then, leaving these reflections behind, they stepped out into the city under its blanket of smog. An accordionist warmed his fingers on a first tune, harvesting mocking glances from creatures who had been born into more sanitary conditions but wouldn't recognise a high C if it slapped them in the face. That's if they accorded the accordionist the humanity of a glance. Mostly they just ignored him, the good-for-nothing loafer, leaving his hat empty. But this was a dream and people looked his way.

After that, things started to speed up in Ohanna's sleep, growing more exciting, and she climbed onto a bus that was waiting for her in the Rue du Peuple: a bright red city bus, designed for tourists in a hurry. The keys were in the ignition. Jesus went up onto the top floor and Ohanna did the driving; she was as surprised as anyone that she could, swerving between the other vehicles on the permanently clogged inner ring as the drivers beeped and waved their fists and gave her the finger. And just as the sea had once parted for the Lord, all the traffic lights now turned green.

In the Rue Van Gaver she grabbed her microphone and said, 'On Your left, Lord, you see deceived girls, lured to the West by the promise of human rights and now stranded, washed up on this shore like so much driftwood, wreckage from a ship that was given up as lost long ago. To survive they have to take it in every orifice. On Your right, exactly the same thing.'

She drove Him to the Rue Bodeghem so he could feel the Salvation Army's coarse but welcome blankets. She showed him the slums of Marollen, houses where mushrooms do better than people, and the car park on the Boulevard du Jardin Botanique so He could see how the homeless get their beauty sleep by sliding in under a freshly parked car to enjoy the warmth of its engine. Then she led the Good Shepherd along the gloomy canal, whose bed has been fertilised with the body of many a despairing suicide and beside which the city's famous *gueuze* is brewed, to the Boulevard du Neuvième de ligne, home to an asylum seekers' centre and possibly, by consequence, Brussels' most famous avenue, globally speaking.

This was where the dream changed into a nightmare. Jesus tore off his mask, revealing himself as a local government inspector. He roared, 'Ha, where'd you get the gall to give Christ such a distorted picture of Brussels? You haven't said a word about the magnificence of the Chinese Pavilion, not a letter about the great Maison Delune, Horta's buildings, the grandeur of the Parc du Cinquantenaire, the riches we amassed on the backs of all the people we slaughtered in our colonies, our chocolatiers, our chips, the fashionable boutiques on the Place du Grand Sablon . . .' The longer Ohanna stared at the unmasked face, the more convinced she became that it belonged to no-one less than the Devil himself, a role some people believe comes naturally to government inspectors.

'Thanks for services rendered, but you're no longer of any use to this country. Your room in Transit Centre 127 is ready and waiting.'

★

Ohanna woke with a start, dripping with sweat. The multi-jet shower came in handy.

Eighth Station

Belgian stamps have always excelled in two subjects: the portrait of the King and birds, preferably defenceless little winter birds that the man and woman in the street can easily identify with, which naturally does no harm at all to the sales of wooden bird feeders.

Besides stamps, Our Majesty's head also fills the TV screen on New Year's Eve when he reads out his New Year's address to his subjects. Ribbon cutting he leaves increasingly to his son, to make sure he masters the profession of head of state in a timely fashion. Kneading his cranium to the shape of the crown, moulding his backside to fit the cushions of the throne. Despite the ever-increasing numbers of prophets of doom whispering that the end of the nation is at hand and that the whole dynasty will soon be moving out of the palace and into a hovel.

My whole life, I've read the slogan BELGIË BARST —

daubed on our public bricks by people who feel strength-ened by the persuasiveness of alliteration – but Belgium hasn't burst apart or gone to hell, despite the dedication of all those graffiti-spraying activists. It has survived five thorough-going reforms of the state, withstood many identity crises and much introspection, floundered through two world wars and endured various separatist movements . . . to more or less preserve the form that was cast by Philip the Good four centuries *before* the kingdom's actual foundation. Belgium is geography's hypochondriac: the State that is convinced it won't last much longer and consequently invests in itself with the greatest of reluctance, as a result of which, given that it *does* continue to exist, it perseveres as a shambling, invariably backward nation that has invested too little in itself.

Of course Belgium will one day cease to exist and be replaced by something else that won't last forever either. Longevity is reserved for the sponges, but they too will one day be obliterated.

And so it was that year after year we had felt a certain hesitation when marking the celebration of our nationhood on the calendar (the twenty-first of July, that's right, the date on which, in 1831, our first king – a German – had taken his less-than-whole-hearted oath).

★

Christ's planning His coming for our national holiday bitterly offended our fatherland-haters, who saw it as misplaced meddling by an omnipotent being who had no business getting involved in earthly politics. If *Homo sapiens* hadn't been Creation's manufacturing error in the first place, the Saviour wouldn't have been in a position to gloat over His progeny's form of government anyway. All at once republicans revealed the depth of their biblical knowledge by grumbling that Jesus's choice for the twenty-first of July had nothing to do with His sympathies for the Belgian royals, and everything to do with the opposite. Because just as He had once astutely pointed out to Pontius Pilate that the true King had Mary as his mild mother and grew up among the shavings of a carpenter who was not his begetter, so Christ was now descending to the open sewers of Brussels to draw the attention of the King of the Belgians, aka Grand Master of the Order of Malta, Grand Master of the Order of Leopold II and Knight of the Danish Order of the Elephant, to his complete incompetence as a monarch . . .

Blah, blah.

And once again, blah.

But even if you had ideological objections to monarchy as a form of government, considered the notion of the sceptre passing to someone who had simply inherited it medieval, and couldn't stomach the idea of the Crown being protected at all times – even if you were horrified by the enormous subsidies poured each year into the tomatoes in the royal greenhouses just to maintain a symbol – you still had little difficulty in admitting that the monarch was probably a great bloke. I say 'probably' because, of course, you didn't know him personally. Anyone who wanted to get to know the King had to move to a flood-prone area or survive a train crash. But then, assuming your first impressions were rendered more reliable by a life richly filled with human contacts, you would be very likely to admit that our monarch was pleasant company. Speaking for myself, I would not have had any objections to dining with him. He was, if I've judged his character correctly, essentially a dead ordinary softy, a person like you or me who secretly reached into the frying pan at home with his dirty fingers. A cheerful sneak, skilled in the unnoticed filching of chocolates, creative when it came to unearthing occasions on which to drink an extra glass of wine. A person with bowel movements so troublesome that he often didn't leave the toilet until the newspaper ink had penetrated his knees. Unlike the ancient skalds, our poets should present our king as a gentleman with endearing failings, a supply of slightly risqué jokes he could draw on to accompany a *digestif*, a hearing aid, high cholesterol. Someone who had had his indiscretions and felt remorse for the heartache it had caused his wife, the Queen, a former model who was now showing a little too much craquelure. But the King was not the kind of person who would show us up in front of Christ – the commission members in the priory of Val-Duchesse reached agreement on that too, just before the crème brûlée was served.

You see, practical considerations alone were enough to convince everyone that it was far easier to celebrate both Christ and our worldly king at the same time. If the parades in honour of the two of them took the same route, there would be no need to close extra streets to traffic unnecessarily, and enough parking meters would be left operative and generating income. Accordingly the committee decided to locate the lion's share of the festivities on the route the military parade traditionally followed on the twenty-first of July: the Place Poelaert, the Rue de la Régence, the Sablon, the Place Royale. Christ could, for example – this was just a first draft – be driven in a special vehicle with a bubble of bullet-proof glass all the way up to the stage where the royal family was waiting for Him on the seats of honour. Although it was questionable whether a country with a national debt of 296 billion euros should invest heavily in the security of someone who was immortal. Of course not. An assassination attempt on the Messiah was the most ridiculous thing a terrorist could come up with. So, here we go, a second draft. Christ could ride in a sedan chair, the papal Sedia Gestatoria . . . Yes, that was more ceremonial, carried up to the King and, not forgetting, Ohanna. Or we'd let Him ride a young ass – rumour had it He was a dab hand at that. Afterwards, the two guests of honour could watch the parade of marching cannon fodder – *for unity we'd die a hero's death* – followed by a procession of stilt-walkers, as if to assuage any fears that life might not be worth living if you've had a leg shot off. The gendarmerie brass band, founded to prove that a ticket writer can also grasp the rudiments of music, would blast a hymn through their bombardons, with the Moha majorettes in their wake. Then a squadron of F-16s would fly over the heads of the many invitees in formation: a cross, for instance. If we could be so bold as to uphold tradition, a detachment of the local police, comprised of a Volkswagen Jetta from police district Sint-Truiden and an inconspicuous Skoda from the district La Louviére, would then proceed through the capital. Followed by a detachment of the federal police flaunting a Peugeot 807 from the Canine Support Service and an Opel Vivaro from the lab of the federal court police in Tournai. To stop the Lord from nodding off completely, there'd be some thunderous fireworks next, with loud church music

74

evoking a theatrical scene from the Old Testament. Again, it was just a suggestion.

It was clear, more thought was required.

Maybe a good idea to put out some feelers with an event organiser?

As tentative as the details of the programme were, the announcement of the route caused an unambiguous outburst of joy in Brussels Park, where masses of the Lord's most tenacious fans had set up their tents, leaving me unsure as to whether I should compare the overpopulated space to a festival field or a refugee camp in Darfur. And to think that all this hysteria had been started by one old lady on a folding chair on the pavement. The authorities had trucked in Portaloos, but these proved unable to swallow the vast quantities quickly enough, which was unpleasant for anyone with open footwear. Depositing the final product of one's digestive system in a bush was far preferable, even if the space given over to shrubbery in this park was nowhere near enough to provide cover for more than a week to thousands, no, tens of thousands of believers' bowel movements. The man who had climbed up into one of the park's many trees – soon known as Zacchaeus – was determined to hold on to his fabulous lookout post; he accepted the food and water passed up by volunteers and took the easy way out by shitting shamelessly in his pants. On the day itself the branch on which he was sitting would be the *nec plus ultra* of any real estate agent and would undoubtedly bring many times more than flat residents in, say, Monaco could get for renting out a square metre of balcony when the Formula One cars were tearing through their fiscal Valhalla. Fortunately the eating stalls that had sprung up everywhere – chips, *escargots*, hot dogs . . . the usual suspects – disseminated smells strong enough to take up the gauntlet and combat the reek of ammonia.

A holiday feeling was in the air.

Ninth Station

Suddenly my summer morning rituals included wandering
past a few different newspaper stands to give myself the
pleasure of seeing just how much my home town had magne-
tised international media outlets. Brussels adorned the front
pages of all the world's leading magazines. Not one rolled off
the presses without bestowing attention on our attractions.
Hot tips for gourmets, special destinations for shopping
addicts, the charm of tram 44 with Het Spoorloos Café as the
last stop, alternative accommodation for those who hadn't
been able to book a bed in a hotel or found the prices for the
few beds that were still available totally prohibitive, establish-
ments where you could get an authentic beer with a beautiful
head on it . . . topics all editors everywhere were willing to
throw money at. For the umpteenth time in its rich history,
Time magazine put Jesus on the cover but – and this was a first
– now as a visitor to Brussels' Grand Place, which is, after

all, without any blind chauvinism, one of the most beautiful squares on the whole planet. Dark and gloomy, but beautiful. As a result, the number of Americans who think of Brussels as the capital of Bulgaria must have plummeted towards zero and if anyone should have thanked Jesus for so much free publicity, it was this city's tourist industry. Every day I bought two foreign newspapers with a Brussels monument on the front page, preferably written in a language of which I did not understand a single syllable. As souvenirs. Me, who had always found it difficult to restrain my smirks when Veronique hoarded mementoes, filling scrapbooks with concert and subway tickets, locks of hair, notes we'd left each other, boarding passes.

I was standing at our front door with the *Helsingun Sanomat* and the *Tokyo Shimbun* under one arm when the upstairs neighbour patted me on the back and said, 'So, Dutch isn't enough to keep yourself informed any more?' And this in such a jovial tone that he might just as well have preceded his remark with a term of address like 'old buddy'. What made this scene so special, however, was that my neighbour had never wearied his vocal cords on my account before. In the most favourable instances, he had jerked his chin up as a form of greeting, invariably resembling a seal in those brief moments, but whenever able to avoid eye contact, he'd refrained from that bloodless twitch as well. I only knew he was called Antoine because it was written on the doorbell, because the postman occasionally put his letters in my letter-box by mistake and because a woman had once stood on the landing at three in the morning screaming his name at the top of her voice, followed by the demand, 'At least let me get my clothes!'

'Potato peelings can't read!' I blurted. A feeble comeback, I know, but reasonably witty for me.

He then asked me if I was on holiday yet.

Yes, I was.

'And the woman you live with too?'

Yes, Veronique too.

'Would you like to come to dinner at my place this evening, the two of you?'

This city, like many others, was a place where you could spend years living under the same roof, clustered around the same lift shaft, without getting to know each other. If there was a gas explosion, Antoine and I would be lamented in the same book of condolence, the news of our demise would be printed on the same sheet of newspaper and the chances were high that we would remain neighbours in the municipal cemetery until the leases on our burial plots expired. But that shared fate was too insignificant to bring us together. Until then I'd only known his voice as it sounded through walls and floors, and suddenly he was addressing me, following one sentence with another and even inviting me up for a meal. These truly were mad days.

To be honest, I'd never felt disadvantaged by being able to dissolve into a crowd and I'd often preferred the straight-forward anonymity of the city to the hypocritical arts villagers master to sustain their mutual greetings year after year. Perhaps it was because I was a city boy through and through – the only rabbits I'd ever seen had been skinned and had a barcode on their bum — but the prospect of a neighbour keeping tabs on my comings and goings was anything but a comfort. If I realised while preparing dinner that I'd run out of butter, I wouldn't knock on my neighbour's door to ask if I could borrow a pat ('Ten grams is enough, I'll make sure to bring it back tomorrow.'). I'd rather throw together a completely different meal from yesterday's leftovers. If neces-sary, I'd make a virtue of necessity and pull on my coat to go out and treat myself to a plate somewhere – bangers and mash at Café de l'Opera, and a full glass of Gigondas. What am I saying? A carafe! And yes, I did claim earlier in this modest chronicle that, of all liquids, I only tipped beer and coffee down my gullet, but now you know that I wasn't being

entirely honest at that stage. Anyway, butter, Gigondas . . .
Any right-minded person would start hoping they'd run out
of butter again sometime very soon. But good neighbours
were people who bent over backwards to make sure they
hardly even existed for *their* neighbours – that remained my
firm belief.

Just under six hours later, for want of a decent excuse,
Veronique and I crossed the doormat of someone who had
shared the intimacy of his nocturnal coughing fits with us, a
man we heard flush every few hours, and astonishingly I felt
very pleased with myself for making the acquaintance of
a neighbour, something that allowed me to go out in my
slippers and drink a few glasses too many, yet remain within
crawling distance of my own front door.

So, there I was. Initially I had been annoyed when people
started storing their music in invisible files on iPods and other
devices. It deprived me of the luxury of standing in front of
a shelf full of CDs or LPs and immediately having something
to talk about. 'Oh, you into that?' Or, 'Great, this. I love it too.
I saw her last year live with her band at the Ancien Belgique
. . . What? You were there too? Really . . .' A way of warming
up the conversation. The same fate lay in store for books.
Complete libraries now fitted onto a chip the size of a

fingernail; increasingly, you needed to pull out a computer to follow the route of someone's intellectual education. In my lifetime, at least during the first and most supple part of it, I had generally got to know people in front of bookcases – and CD racks – and I found it a terrible loss that new technology had deprived me of this ice-breaker, this social and intellectual point of orientation. So I went over to the window to look out at a view that was almost identical to my own. 'We can't complain about where we live,' I said to have something to say, gazing out at the busy city. But Antoine picked up the thread and in two shakes we were conversing about the many blessings of our location: the cinemas, the comic shops, Joseph Niels's excellent minced beef and the unsympathetic price he unfortunately, more than unfortunately, asked for it, the concert venues, the theatres, the art galleries, the nesting falcons on the cathedral towers, the accounts of Ohanna's dreams we read in our newspapers, the busker who had been occupying a spot in Metro Madou for five weeks now and displayed such talent that it seemed an injustice that this man who smelt of rollmops wasn't on stage at the Cirque Royal . . .

I had also been relieved to see Antoine open a bag of crisps to munch with the drinks. The whole rage of calling a chicory leaf dipped in mayonnaise an amuse-bouche was way too snooty for me: when people started talking about food in trendy, pompous terms, I always felt they were being dishonest. To me, zakuskis are and will always be open-faced sandwiches, I prefer snacks to tapas, and a smoothie is nothing more or less than a pulped cucumber. Surely? It was simply a question of sincerity: someone who already felt the urge to hide the simplicity of the pre-dinner nibbles behind buffed and polished words wouldn't hesitate to smear a deceitful layer of language over themselves as well. As far as that went, I welcomed the jocular way our neighbour ripped open the bag of crisps as a candid declaration of a genuine wish to get to know us. Unmasked, I mean.

Plain salted crisps, no better kind.

During the meal – a forgotten classic: chicken with apple sauce, and I have to stop writing about food or the drool will drip down onto the letters of my keyboard – I found it easy to accept the idea that the purpose of Christ's imminent arrival was to revive interest in His Eucharistic message. Bringing people together around a carafe of grape juice and a lump of bread – a truly noble goal and, according to my modest knowledge of the Bible, the quintessence of the New Testament. It could have been the wine (one and a half bottles a head leads to completely new insights), but suddenly I also understood the meaning of that inspirational line that sweetens children's voices in tubercular churches: 'For in wine and in bread, I break free of death.' I, too, as a six-year-old communicant, had thrown all of the enthusiasm I had in me into this song in the minutes preceding the disillusionment concerning the cardboard taste of the host, yelling every letter of the missal text up into the rood loft as if my life depended on it. Of course I didn't have the foggiest what it meant. And make no mistake: I don't understand it now either, not at all. And I wouldn't know what there was to understand about it. But there, at Antoine's table, gnawing a drumstick, I did. Again, it was all that wine, you have to take that into account.

I feel uncomfortable raking up the memory of that moment and would prefer to ignore the event completely. But if I kept silent about it, I wouldn't be properly conveying that period that was so full of expectation. So here it comes: I couldn't resist speaking that particular sentence at my neighbour's dinner table. Out loud, yes indeed. Like that woman in the tram who had spoken a sentence out loud a few days earlier. I can still hear myself saying *'For in wine and in bread, I break free of my death.'* Pleased with myself for having managed to wrest a line of a hymn out of the grip of oblivion. Veronique laid down her fork and looked at me. I could be grateful that no-one had choked on their apple sauce. But before I had time to bemoan my own impulsivity, even before I had readied myself to be the brunt of Veronique's scornful laughter, she took up the baton for me. '. . . *God in Heaven extends us His hand.*' And the next thing, all three of us were sitting around the carcass of a chicken singing the whole song. And by singing, I mean at the top of our lungs. '*Lord, Lord, take this gift, take my self, all my dreams, all I've planned.*' It was a cheerful song, really. Or at least, the melody was written by a carefree composer. Whether they were still ramming it into the heads of the latest batch of lambs to be Christianised, I didn't know. But Belgians my age, who learnt the Hail Mary before the alphabet, know this song. More than that, it's a musical milestone in their existence. The more I think about it, the less plausible I find it that I sat there singing cheerful hymns with the neighbour I had, until very recently, never said a word to. Like fanatical Catholic teenagers who merrily psalmodise the sunset at religious camps, united in their pride at having renounced sex before marriage. That was us. Never will I be able to eat chicken with apple sauce again without thinking back on that mad moment.

If Veronique and I had followed the regular rhythm of our calendar, we would have been somewhere very far away, with or without a mosquito net draped over us, in a country that made us feel like travellers, not tourists. As always, we would have been glad to leave the commercial belt around the hotel as quickly as possible to immerse ourselves in the lives of what are generally known as the common people. The price of our plane tickets was wasted money unless we spent at least one evening of our stay in the company of a local, someone who didn't have a thing to do with the tourist industry. Like every other cocky globetrotter and purchaser of so-called alternative travel guides, we had no greater goal than getting off the beaten track. But what right had we had to dedicate all that summertime travelling to the pursuit of authenticity? Weren't we guilty of a form of snobbery when we supported our story addiction in Kenya with the tales of an anonymous basket weaver but hadn't even said hello to our very own neighbour back home?

See: we'd stayed home and we had our authenticity. We were listening to a man, an IT specialist as it turned out, a card-carrying member of a squash club, a keen chess player and, as such, regularly to be found bent over a board in the famous Greenwich Taverne, romantically unattached, and a murderer.

Assuming that he had just told a joke and wanting to hide my failure to get it, I laughed.

It was time, he said, that he confessed the black stain on

his soul. Of course, it was the coming of the Almighty that had got him thinking. He'd been bothered by remorse before, true, often, but this time he couldn't postpone his confession any longer. He had to let it out! He'd lost his faith in the Church, no surprise there, so he'd decided to confess his terrible sin to a neighbour. For God, that would be as good as a priest.

'What do you mean?' I asked.

'I murdered my wife!'

'The one who was on the stairs once without any clothes . . .'

'You don't know her. The offence dates from some time ago, plus I was living somewhere else at the time . . . She got on my nerves, it's true, but that's what divorce is for, to counteract murder. Anyway, this is my confession: I murdered someone, laid her in the bath and then set fire to the house. Until now I have unjustly enjoyed the pity of friends and family who grieve with me because I lost my wife in tragic circumstances. I still get weekly phone calls from my then parents-in-law, lamenting the fact that their daughter died before leaving them the consolation of a troop of grandchildren . . .'

★

You can expect many things when you're invited to a meal somewhere for the first time, but this scenario – 'dinner by artificial light in the home of a repentant Judas' was beyond my powers of imagination. I regretted not having any serious transgressions of my own to make things a little more mutual. Really, having something to confess to would have been very convenient. If not a murder, at least a carjacking or something like that. Unfortunately my last theft only involved a Raider chocolate bar. And I'd already confessed that forty years earlier – when it had never occurred to anyone that the brand Raider would one day cease to exist – in the Notre-Dame du Finistère confessional to a priest who seemed to have dozed off. So all we could do was thank our neighbour for his candour and the faith he'd shown in us.

'You've never thought of going to the police?' – Veronique with a brave but pertinent question.

'The prisons are full, you know that as well as I do. Here in Brussels you can empty the magazine of a pistol into a passing bus and get away with an ankle bracelet and some psychotherapy. And what if the judges do prove willing to honour my crime with a camp bed in a cell? Would it make me a better man? Every jailer admits it: you go into prison a criminal and come out a gangster. My Righteous Judge lies ahead. I'm ready for Him. *Sooner or later God's going to cut you down.*'

And because he declaimed that last bit solemnly in an American accent, I unquestioningly assumed he had it from some song or other.

Crazy days, I can't say that enough.

Tenth Station

One can safely assume that not a single embryo has a say in its place of birth. My hailing from Brussels and Belgium is no achievement and if I'm honest there's never been any love lost between me and those who flaunt their nationality as a mark of distinction, a status they obtained simply by being lucky enough to see the light of day in a place with superior geographical coordinates. I'm the harmless loon who dreams quietly of a world without nationalities, without flags. Of a world without passports, like the one that existed before the First World War. Or a world without money . . . that too. And if I take it to its logical conclusion, I'm afraid I have to admit that in the broadest sense, I dream of a world without people. Don't get me wrong, I'm comfortable in my fabulous Belgian biotope, surrounded by things and values I love: meatballs à la Liégeoise, the right to journalistic and artistic freedom, asparagus with butter and boiled eggs in May, the fact that not a single woman here has to abort her unwanted child over a toilet bowl with a dirty knitting needle, the cycling obsession on all sides when the spring races are coming up, the existence of a financial safety net for the unemployed ... But I'm not beyond the influence of my upbringing and I'm not beyond the influence of my culture. If I'd been born in the highlands of Papua New Guinea, I'd praise the convenience of a penis gourd! I think. And for that matter, if I had to prove my credentials as a *Brusselaar* by tucking into a piece of authentic Brussels no-fat cheese, also known as *ettekeis* (stinking gunge if you ask me, fresh puke from a diseased and dying dog – but a delicacy according to others), well, I'd fail the test. I could tell my examiners that this so-called cheese, an imitation of a washed-up jellyfish, is manufactured in the Galgstraat, a street named after a gallows, of all things, and I could easily dig up various other pieces of information concerning this product of culinary sadomasochism, but spooning even the slightest bit into my mouth to prove my origins: never! It's the kind of thing people call an acquired taste. And that generally says it all.

But my aversion to origin-claiming, barricade-manning loudmouths is the reason I've always appreciated being Belgian. Because through the country's whole tricoloured history it's been possible to be an enthusiastic Belgian without having to make a show of it. A country where you never have to be a proud singer of the national anthem. Where I've never known anyone who was really interested in producing a fault-less rendition of the country's chosen ditty. Maybe our three official languages get in the way. There is such a tendency for it to descend into a cacophony when the members of a crowd begin simultaneously praising the fatherland in their own mother tongues. With the exception of a few oddballs, I have never heard a soul warble the complete lyrics of our anthem, and that's fabulous. On the increasingly rare occasions that our national football team manages to qualify for a champi-onship, the ceremonial section preceding the defeat makes it clear that neither the players nor the supporters are able to do any better than sly humming. Or they simply replace the words with 'la, la, la'. Yes, we la-la-la the Brabançonne en masse and it has always struck me as absolutely logical for us to talk about ourselves in those same Dadaistic terms. Believe me, I've always counted myself lucky to be a resident of a realmlet that has 'la la la la la la la la la la la la . . . la la la . . .' as the unofficial lyrics of its national anthem. It could hardly be more cheerful. And you can't say that about yodelling that our fatherland has an inalienable right to the blood flowing through our veins, as required by the actual libretto.

Italians call on each other to unite in cohorts, ready for

death. Armenians bellow that death is the same for everyone, but only he who dies for his country is happy. The Cypriots like to compare themselves to a sword that makes everyone who sees it tremble. It casts the formal parts of international sporting events in a particularly sombre light. Give me that friendly la la la of ours anytime, at least it doesn't reek of war.

La la la, a pint at the bar.

As a result I was all the more horrified when, a few years ago, this country's northerners suddenly remembered the words of their regional song and began seizing every opportunity to sing it. Check it yourself sometime: whenever there's an increase in the chanting of a national anthem in this or that history, mankind is once again about to demonstrate that its level of civilisation is far from praiseworthy. Wars have begun more often with a song than a bang. I just couldn't believe that those prosperous people in the north with all their luxuries and mod cons had embraced a dated composer heart and soul and were now blaring the heroic deeds of a metaphorical lion. A lion that *ripped, destroyed and smashed apart, got drenched with gore and mud, and then, in triumph, grinned upon its dead foe's flowing blood.* Beautiful lines, bravo. But more and more political parties were concluding their congresses or electoral speeches with this song. I could only feel vicarious shame at the sight of grown people – contemporaries and compatriots – losing themselves in this folkloric rhetoric. And given half a chance, they completed the patriotic kitsch by waving their flag, which was an ugly flag, designed by someone who was colour-blind, in glaring yellow and black, showing a furious lion lashing out with the claws with which the self-satisfied part of the population, ready to tear themselves away as a nation of the self-satisfied alone, apparently identified. Someone seeing this flag for the first time would have sworn it was a pirate's flag made by children who had not yet outgrown this kind of whimpering heroism and needed to defend their tree huts and secret encampments with the symbols boys' own adventure stories use to exorcise the boredom of a long summer's day. I was staggered by the speed with which something so ridiculous could become generally accepted. Hardly anyone seemed disturbed by this viral *Blut und Boden* cult, hardly anyone was visibly scared. And those who were disturbed and scared were labelled quislings in letters to editors and all kinds of virtual cesspits for Internet opinions, people who had fouled their own nest and should be tarred and feathered. *Woe on him*, in other words, and I will now sing the whole farce, *that false and faithless foe, who strokes the Flemish Lion, then aims a traitor's blow* . . .

A nation beating its chest in front of the mirror.

The whole mechanism, perfect for pitting large groups

of people against each other, had been set in motion. You could see the wheels turning.

I have to admit that the squabbling between the different communities had dropped off a little in this period. Until, that is, the question was spoken out loud: which hymn should be used to welcome Christ on the tarmac (because everyone still assumed that He would land at either Zaventem or Melsbroek airport, if only to honour Belgian industry by dragging His sandals over five hundred metres of locally produced red carpet)? As far as anyone knew, heaven did not have an official anthem. But the Flemish militants, with memories trained by countless TV quizzes, immediately recalled the third verse of their lion song, a verse that recounted how for thousands of years the king of the beasts had fought for land, liberty and God – *and* God, exactly – and proposed welcoming Him with the bombastic tones of this paean to their own willingness to serve.

Of course, singing your own praises isn't the most hospitable way of welcoming someone, and fortunately the organisers in the Val-Duchesse nerve centre soon came to that realisation.

Under time pressure and tormented by their long-cultivated disdain for all things literary, the committee felt obliged to turn to the public for help. An appeal went out to the amateur poets of all provinces asking them to glue their backsides to their office chairs and come up with some lines that could serve as a singable greeting to the Lord. Professional authors were allowed to display their talents as well, of course, inasmuch as they might prove useful to society for a change. But many among them, godless almost by definition, had expressed themselves so often with such subversive nonsense in the past that the conclave of ministers was much more sympathetic to the idea of handing the pen to the man or woman in the street. It was not only more sympathetic, it was more appropriate to the occasion. But – and this they wanted to emphasise – the competition was open to everyone, every citizen of this country, regardless of language, colour, religion or anything at all. A statement whose chief purpose was avoiding a close encounter with the lawyers of the Centre for Equal Opportunities and Opposition to Racism. Anyway, the welcome song . . . Contestants had to bear the guest's dignity in mind and make sure to use appropriate language. Given the festive nature of the song, a verse-chorus structure was recommended. The masses, generally short on wisdom, also needed to be taken into account. In other words, the lyrics needed to be designed to encourage a spontaneous sing-along and should remain comprehensible for Mother Nature's cerebrally challenged specimens. When choosing their words, authors could consider the timbre – some vowels being easier to sing than others; an *ee*, for instance, is more injurious to the vocal cords than something like an *ah* – but should realise at the same time that much would be lost in translation. Because that too had already been decided: the song would be translated into all of Belgium's national languages plus Latin *and* Aramaic by the Catholic University's brightest students, which meant that aficionados of neologisms could forget about it immediately. The poem was allowed to be of a reasonable length – there was no reason to test Christ's patience with a sonnet cycle, but a haiku might give the impression that we didn't have so very much to say to Him. All entries had to be submitted under pseudonyms, the copyright would be vested in the State, there would be no correspondence of any kind with the jury (which still had to be cobbled together) and all verses needed to reach the letterbox of the Royal Albert Library by the fifteenth of July at the latest (the postmark would be taken as proof, so it was to be hoped that the postal services didn't institute yet another round of savage restructuring that exhausted the staff even more for even less money, because then their employees would go on strike and the contestants would have to take their letters to Brussels themselves). The winner would be announced immediately on all public channels during the evening news of the seventeenth of July and, besides the honour and the TV fame, they would also have a street in Brussels named after them. Conveniently, there was one left that they'd forgotten to name until now, a narrow cobbled side street off the Rue de la Révolution that didn't lead anywhere and was particularly popular with adulterous sneaks and men with tiny bladders.

The melody would be entrusted to . . . Well, that hadn't been fully decided yet, but in any case, it would be a professional, someone who was up to producing a composition suitable for choirs, carillons, bombardons and street organs in less than three days.

A street name, an illusion of immortality, that was all it took to get half the population writing doggerel. Vanity – Pope Gregory I may have seen it as one of the cardinal vices, but my timorously concealed ambition to one day weld a few unforgettable sentences together let itself be lured out of the corner where it had been hidden for years. Veronique too suddenly recalled that at school she'd always got her best marks for composition and happily gave herself a sporting chance. According to the website she consulted, possible rhymes for Jesus included cheeses, diseases, sneezes, tweezers and geezers. She scribbled the words down on a bread bag and tried out a few sentences.

And by the way: was that our neighbour we could hear, the murderer, clacking away on an old typewriter? The romantic!

It would have shown a lack of self-criticism if I'd begun preparing myself for a literary triumph, but so many surprises had rained down recently that one more wouldn't have shocked me. So yes, despite my greeting-card rhymes, I was, in all my naivety, still counting on a more-than-miraculous outcome and, come the seventeenth of July, hanging on every word Ophélie Fontana, the news reader on duty, said. I heard the neighbour turn up his television too, and when I looked out of the window I was struck by how quiet the street was. The winning poem of welcome for the Lord, said Ophélie, after a report on the thirteenth stage of the Tour de France and an item on a football transfer, paid attention to subjects that meant a lot to Christ himself. The weak. The rejected. The lame. It appealed for charity and solidarity, cohabitation, love and justice. So much so that the expert snoopers of the investigation brigade smelt a rat. And, apparently, not without reason. The winning poem, submitted under the pseudonym Freddie Freeloader, was a plagiarism. More precisely, it was nothing but a series of snippets copied from reference books in Aurora, the socialist library on the Avenue Jean Volders. To avoid further offence, a decision had now been made to abandon this poetic appeal to the populace – with sincere apologies for all the pointless effort people had put in – and simply welcome Christ with the words He Himself had taught His apostles: the Our Father, a prayer that was thankful, beseeching, professing and welcoming all at once, sung by a select group of virtuoso sacristans, with the support of the complete lung capacity of the Cramique Brass Band.

'Involving the people in the festivities? My fucking arse!' I heard echoing through our stairwell. And it occurred to me that it had been days, if not weeks, since I had heard someone swear. And how I had missed that hearty beauty.

Eleventh Station

Clearing out my mother's apartment was much more daunting than I'd imagined. The mere thought of rummaging through her drawers and opening her wardrobes to decide what was ready for the tip and what deserved a delay of execution felt extremely rude. I dreaded having to bag her underwear and pick up each of her hats while asking myself out of politeness and politeness alone whether I shouldn't keep one of them as a souvenir. Because obviously I already knew that I didn't like any of those hats. And I didn't have a trunk full of fancy dress articles back home that needed restocking.

A chansonnier once sang himself into the Top Ten with the words '*I won't be dead until you've forgotten me*' and at the time everyone said, 'You have to play this later at my funeral!' Perhaps my sudden recollection of that particular song had something to do with my discomfort, because although none of those material mementoes could bring my mother back, I still felt like each object I threw into the rubbish bin would make her deader than she already was.

I removed the batteries from her four wall clocks, not so much as a symbolic act, but because the ticking was getting me down.

My mother's drawers: filled with lace tablecloths for the guests she hadn't had for a good twenty years, spare batteries for all her click-clacking clocks, envelopes, the sugar cubes and individually wrapped biscuits she'd smuggled out of coffee shops in her handbag like the impoverished wretch in a yet-to-be-discovered manuscript by Charles Dickens, a box of stamps dating from the days when the Belgian franc still existed; filled with Sunday-best handkerchiefs, telegrams announcing the deaths of people nobody had thought about for years. In her kitchen cupboards I found some thirty glasses all told, whereas she always drank out of one and the same glass: the simplest one, stained with scale from the tap water.

Maybe there were some beers left in the fridge? Ultimately the refrigerator needed emptying too, didn't it? This clearing out of mine had to start somewhere. And it was good that I'd hit on this thirst-quenching notion now and not three or so weeks later. The mould on the cheeses was already a horrific sight. Blue, green, woolly. In other words: just the thing for gourmets of the kind you'd find among the ranks of *ettekeis* fanatics.

Who would have looked the most disgusting at that moment: my mother or the cheeses she'd left her son and heir?

Listlessness threatened. I slumped down in my mother's armchair and stared out at the cow. It stood there as alone as my mum had been sitting here, as alone as many elderly people are in big cities. Remembering – that was all I had to do in these rooms. Until I had emptied them and could hand the keys over to the landlord, close this door behind me for ever and go out into the world as an orphan for the time that was left me. And though I made an effort to round off my mother's life by hauling up as many beautiful moments as possible out of the well of forgetting, nothing came.

Incapable of making a selection of her possessions (no vase or scarf I could become attached to), I decided not to make a selection at all. Everything had to go. Every last thing. A short, sharp shock. And I hurried out onto the pavement – where everyone smiled at me and said hello, where nobody pretended to be in a hurry or feared I might be a murderer when I spoke to them – and asked if anyone was interested in a kitchen cupboard, totally free of charge, a mattress, a saucepan, a coffeepot . . .

Birds chirp an alert to their fellow birds when they spot bread crumbs in a garden and people have been signalling each other for a while now by text message. In no time it was open house at my mother's. A to-and-fro of families who had been forced to struggle that little bit harder to make ends meet – often because they had reproduced that little bit more – and were still grateful for second-hand towels or a dilapidated side table. Women tried on dressing gowns in the bathroom, handymen took the bed apart, disconnected the chandeliers and helped each other carry the heavier pieces down the stairs. If only she'd known, my old mum, that her clothes would one day be worn by Moroccans, Congolese, Uzbeks, Afghanis; her sheets slept on by couples who had fled distant regions but still missed them deeply! And as I tried to imagine my mother's face as she watched her furnishings being shared out among all those who had terrified her during her life, I couldn't stop my gob from taking on an amused smile. Men and women I had known only as silent sliding figures in our shared asphalt landscape now offered me their sincerest condolences. They thanked me for my generosity and invited me to drop by for tea.

Fruitful are the days on which one makes friends.

★

Despite having anticipated several afternoons' worth of lifting and lugging, a backbone that reminded me how old I was and innumerable drives to the city's rubbish processers with the debris from smashed-up wardrobes and cupboards, I had hardly one full trailer to drive to the tip in the Rue du Rupel. I had unexpectedly taken care of this horrible job in just a couple of hours while making quite a few families happier at the same time.

The apartment was empty, a chapter was closed.

How many chapters did I have left?

Veronique called. How far had I got? And had I been listening to the radio?

'How far? Wait for it!' I whooped. 'You won't believe your ears, but the whole place is empty. The landlord has the keys, the deposit's been refunded, it's all taken care of. At this very moment, my mother's curtains are probably in a hard-working housewife's sewing machine being transformed into cushion covers. Her paintings are probably being removed from their frames to be replaced by photos of dark-skinned children. Fantastic, isn't it!'

'Have you been listening to the radio?' she repeated.

'What's on the radio?'

'The news. Early this evening the authorities are going to

start sealing off the inner city. After that no cars will be allowed in or out. It's a security measure. Keeping the city free of traffic will make it easier and they want to guard against car bombs too. So make sure you're back on time otherwise they might not let you into your own neighbourhood . . .'

'Why not? I'm from Brussels, it says so on my ID.'

'That's just it, you left your wallet on the table. You're out on the road without any papers, darling.'

She said *darling*, an atrociously ugly word, and it didn't make me feel uncomfortable.

'What's more, we've been bopping all over town in the car without a valid inspection certificate for more than a month!'

I turned on the car radio and heard someone working their way through a long list of approach roads to the centre of town, in the tone you could hear every workday peak hour on Radio Vivacité. The newsreader then bent over a report that had just come in, a grisly discovery in Courtrai, where a group of nuns had hung themselves in the convent attic. You could just picture it: all those wobbling black skirts containing freshly decomposing nuns, dangling from the rafters. It was the kind of scene that cried out to be painted. Still life with dead nuns.

Of course, the nuns in this news item were members of an order that had come in for some fierce criticism in the recent past. Their lace wimples had inspired many a cartoonist when it was revealed that, several decades earlier, these brides of Christ had sexually abused the orphans who had been entrusted to their care. Testimonies of boys, now damaged men, who were forced to creep under a Mother Superior's musty skirts and lick her hairy gash until she stopped trembling. Eight-year-old girls who were roughly deflowered by the fingers that Sister Clementia had just unclasped from pious prayer, and severely punished if they cried while she was at it. The statement of one person who had been marked for life gave someone else who had also been mistreated the courage to drag their past out from under the carpet too. That got the shitball rolling. An avalanche of horror stories thundered down into the valley of milk and honey, briefly relieving the tabloids of their need to grub around in the sex lives of TV celebrities.

Just after the news of this collective suicide had gone on air, motorists all around me began beeping their horns joyfully and waving to each other, as if we had all been listening to the incredibly gripping radio coverage of a football game in which the Red Devils scored in the final seconds. Those were the days, the rare days when the beeping on the motorway was happy and harmonious.

It was bizarre, but the nuns' suicide – their cheap and cowardly *mea culpa* on the eve of Christ's coming, afraid as they were that this would be the Day of Judgment, the long-predicted Overwhelming Event – was a source of delight that unified everyone and everything, and it was a shame that the news was released before nightfall, because otherwise the sense of justice having been done would have undoubtedly led many to light up the Pleiades with a skyrocket or two.

Sure enough, at the Place Sainctelette all vehicles had to pull over and the drivers had to show their wads of documents. I had no desire to put on a show of rummaging through the glove box before adopting an expression of horror and saying, 'Gosh, that's funny, my papers aren't in here.' Policemen know that act, they see several versions of it every day. So I said straight out that I was out on the streets without any documentation. And that I'd also forgotten to take the car to the garage for the annual inspection. The officer, tormented by a monstrous birthmark on his face (if it had been a Rorschach test, I would have said: a map of Holland!), was as happy as a man in love and seemed incapable of making a fuss about anything. 'I have no reason to doubt it. Of course your papers are in order,' he said, and his breath stank of filthy tobacco, which caused an abrupt decline in the pity I felt because of his birthmark. 'And as far as the inspection goes, if you've forgotten it, you've forgotten it. A bad memory is not a crime. You'll see to it shortly, I'm sure of that.'

I thanked him for being so friendly.

'Don't mention it. Nowadays everyone is honest and friendly to the police. That makes it a lot easier for us to be friendly too. Soon we'll be out of work, ha! Imagine.'

I was allowed to enter the inner city with my car. But only to park it in front of the door and not touch it again until the morning of the twenty-second of July. Until then the centre of Brussels would be car-free, just like that one Sunday in September when our children can taste the rustic pleasure of a game of football on the asphalt and we cough up the soot that has built up in our lungs over the past year and triumphantly cycle and roller-skate through the winding tunnels of the *petite ceinture*. After which the emergency services have so many injuries and broken limbs to deal with that they beg for the immediate reinstatement of King Automobile.

★

I drove into a city, my city, where entire neighbourhoods were profiting from the reduced traffic by organising barbecues in the middle of the avenues. Volleyball nets had been strung up across the breadth of boulevards, with the inhabitants of uneven house numbers taking on those with even numbers. Women cleaned their windows, men painted the house fronts or hung banners from the gutters: 'Salut Jésus, Roi de Bruxelles'. The streets smelt of freesias and there weren't any cigarette butts to be seen on the pavements. Even the rabbis from the main synagogue on the Rue de la Régence – where, according to some, new laws were passed long before the Chamber or Senate considered them – clambered up a ladder with a brush and a tin of paint, Sabbath or no Sabbath, to daub their walls with their own variant: 'Salut Jésus, Roi des Juifs'.

At home Veronique had a cold beer ready. For all the work I'd done.

Rare days. If you'd given me a tune, I'd have whistled it for you – in counterpoint.

Twelfth Station

The twentieth of July was announced as the day on which
the national record for a maximum temperature might be
broken. There was even a possibility of the mercury pushing
up past the magical barrier of forty degrees Celsius for the
first time in our history. In the same tone with which they
had cursed the winter six months earlier, the eternal malcontents now declared how much they were looking forward to
November's frozen chrysanthemums. And, of course, people
were quick to put the dog-day heat down to Christ's coming
rather than blame it on pollution and global warming. Some
drew an association between the soaring temperatures and
the New Testament story of the Pentecostal flames, an undeniably interesting take on things, and proof positive that Jesus
must already be in town. We'd overlooked Him, the Son of
Man had slipped past without our noticing. He was already
here. And as I explained above, since we were living in an age

in which the news of every little fart was endlessly repeated without further verification, each rumour was tweeted, texted, skyped, emailed, pinged, ponged or beeped on old-fashioned car horns if the batteries were flat, and the masses swarmed back and forth through the city according to the latest rumour. If a story that Jesus was located in the topmost sphere of the Atomium had been launched at a particular hour on that day, it would have led within fifteen minutes to an unparalleled popular stampede in the direction of that monument. If someone had then shouted, 'The Son of God is in the Marollen among His peers, the impoverished and the drunken, the lost and the weak,' the crowd would have immediately rushed off, like air after an explosion, and there wouldn't have been a soul left at the base of our famous collection of big steel balls.

Another theory that was suddenly being whispered from ear to ear on that particular twentieth of July was that, just yesterday, Jesus had attended an open meeting in the masonic lodge *Les Vrais Amis de l'Union et du Progrès Réunis*, something He had enjoyed tremendously and which had given Him a more positive view of humanity. Afterwards a ballot for His election as a member was held. Of all the electronic tittle-tattle that did the rounds that day, my personal favourite was the report that, for some time now, Jesus had been staying in Stoclet Palace on the Avenue de Tervueren – often described

as the Jugendstil Taj Mahal, it had a history of offering tempo-
rary lodgings to members of the beautiful people – and that,
what's more, He had been enjoying the company there of
His revered colleague Mohammed, with whom He passed
the time playing Risk. Stories like this were completely crazy,
even for people who believed in miracles, but that didn't stop
the Avenue de Tervueren from being swamped by so many
autograph hounds that the caretaker of that architectural pearl
could only fear for the safety of his building.

Someone who could undoubtedly have contributed a para-
graph or two on the dangers of mass hysteria was the young
guy on the Rue du Marché aux Herbes, a fourth-generation
hippie, coincidentally strolling out of the Galerie Agora,
where he had just purchased a hash pipe. Of course, his
sandals, poncho and wispy beard were the long-time staples
of children's Bible illustration – that makes it partly under-
standable. And the moment the first person recognised the
poor drip as the Saviour and expressed this recognition with
a shriek of delight, the queues in front of the waffle stands
dissolved and the Rue du Marché aux Herbes was engulfed
by his admirers. It made no difference that the young man
denied being the Son of God. He could shout whatever
he liked and however loudly – 'I come from Hamme. I'm a

qualified social worker . . .' – it couldn't avert his fate. From the St Hubert arcade, the Rue de la Montagne, the Rue de la Madeleine, the Rue des Eperonniers, followers came from all directions, hurling themselves at the unfortunate, grabbing him and tearing at him with all their might, shredding his Bob Marley T-shirt and ripping the sandals off his feet. Why? To use them in amulets! And only when he was completely butt-naked did the mob come half to its senses and disperse, resuming the search for the Messiah in other quarters, leaving the poor wretch behind without a word of apology, lying there in his birthday suit on that summery square with its undiminished aroma of sugar and vanilla.

I have been told that the unlucky hippie switched to hard drugs soon after this unpleasant experience, taking to them with such a vengeance that he snorted his brains to mush and now spends the majority of his days in the garden of a psychiatric institution, on the swing, convinced of his own divinity.

The incident showed very clearly, I thought, that the officials responsible for law and order were not ready for this event and unable to guarantee the safety of Christ Our Saviour or those who happened to resemble him. On top of this, the Minister of Defence in our permanent provisional government for business in hand was stuck abroad because the military aircraft on which he was travelling (for private purposes, according to some), a C130, had broken down and was unable to be repaired in time. You couldn't help but wonder who was going to coordinate it all, who would be there to make a decision if things went wrong. For the first time, I felt a creeping sense of doubt. Was it sensible to be physically present along the route tomorrow? Even with the ceremonies taking place a hair's breadth away from my front door, it might be more advisable to follow it all on TV. A commercial channel had acquired the exclusive rights. Every fifteen minutes you'd have to sit through ads for deodorants, lady shaves or car insurance, but if it meant avoiding having someone rip the clothes off your back, an afternoon in front of the telly was worth considering. When I stopped to think about it, it was no wonder that the commotion in our streets – good-natured still, for now – had been giving me increasingly frequent flashbacks to that balmy spring day in 1985. We were young and proud that our city had been given the privilege of organising the final of the then European Cup. But the collection of dead football fans alongside the pitch, 39 in total, blue, suffocated, trampled, limp sacks that no longer jumped up when Michel Platini kicked his team into the lead . . . Those images have left their mark on the history of Brussels and often come to mind, especially when the masses fill our avenues. I've smelt death in every crowd since.

★

The midday news showed helicopter footage shot around the palace. The fire brigade constantly spraying the crowd. The Red Cross volunteers doing battle with the symptoms of dehydration. Food packages being dropped from a hot-air balloon. In some neighbourhoods people had been crammed together for so long that the weaker ones were already fainting. A fitness guru on top of the statue *Venus with Doves* barked exercise instructions into a megaphone to keep the patient spectators' blood circulating, while a small orchestra in the Vauxhall bandstand fiddled modified keep-fit tunes.

To illustrate just how much the capital had been over-taken by pilgrims, the producers had dispatched camera crews to Belgian holiday destinations as well. The country was deserted. In Bruges the chocolates were going to waste in the window displays, the coachmen's horses were enjoying an unexpected break, the abandoned squares and canals seemed to have been plucked straight from a Fernand Khnopff print. There were no skateboarders or rollerbladers hurtling along the otherwise so busy sea dykes of Blankenberge and Middelkerke; no kites performing arabesques on the breeze, no children glaring at their fallen ice-cream cones, and no customers in the restaurants, despite the heavily discounted seafood menus. The same scenes in the east, where no canoes were scraping their bellies over the rocks of the Amblève and the trout could gulp at the treats the river brought them without fear of fishing lines. The grass in the campgrounds was not being smothered by tents, the people who rented out cottages were suffering losses. And for days now, Théodore Géricault's wonderful *Portrait of a Kleptomaniac* in the Museum of Fine Arts in Ghent had not been visited by a single admirer. The country was empty, and that emptiness suited it wonderfully.

And the coming of the Supreme Being was affecting everyday life in the surrounding countries too: for a week now the Eiffel Tower had been forced to get by with a serious reduction in the number of visitors, extremely serious actually, and the tour-boat companies in Amsterdam's canals were taking advantage of the lull in custom to repair their boats and fish Coke cans out of the water.

Brussels was suffocating. Once this human sea had finally receded, an unsurveyable mass of filth would drive our council workers to despair. You didn't have to be a visionary to see that. All the roads to Brussels Park stank of overripe armpits. Already. Soon we would be hoping for wind, a brisk breeze to blow the sour stench out of our avenues, just as our nineteenth-century predecessors had hoped that the wind would blow cholera away from the streets. But for the time being, all diaries remained blank from the twenty-first of July on. We were totally and single-mindedly focused on that one glorious moment, and that was forgivable.

★

As I mentioned earlier, cars hadn't been allowed into the centre for quite a few hours and the authorities had decided that they should make public transport free as a concession to the countless masses trying to gain access by pressing forward against the hastily erected city walls – that is, the contemporary barbed-wire version of city walls. The Autonomous Train Drivers' Union couldn't have hoped for better news, because if there was *one* choice moment to make a clear statement that their members were under too much pressure, that for some time now there had been no new colleagues appointed to compensate for natural wastage and that the railway security systems were hopelessly obsolete . . . If there was *one* day when they could scream out loud that there were exasperating staff shortages and the authorities' cost-cutting was undermining both the quality of the railways *and* the safety of the passengers, it was now. God Himself as a bargaining chip, a work force didn't get that added to their trade-unionist arsenal every day of the week. It couldn't have been simpler: they called a strike, only their fourth that year.

Unfortunately, inasmuch as the railway staff believed that their demands would be met immediately, given the circumstances, they were badly mistaken. The truth was that everyone, not least of all the mayor, was over the moon that they had called a halt to all that transportation of people. The city needed to be shut off. From now on, only *one* person was going to be allowed in, and that was the Son of God. Hopefully we'd recognise Him.

Everyone else would just have to do what they'd done without protest their whole life long: put their feet up on a pouffe, arrange a bowl of crisps on their track-suited lap, and watch events in complete relaxation on TV.

As it grew darker that evening, an unusual calm descended over the city. Those who believed they had occupied a good viewing spot stuck to their paving stone and refused to budge; the atmosphere around the Grand Place and the Place de la Bourse was subdued. Although the tables in the magically lit Rue des Bouchers were set and there were rumbling stomachs afoot, the hospitality touts from the various restaurants refrained from the folkloristic street theatre they usually deployed to filch each other's customers with rock-bottom prices or the enticement of a free dessert. They looked at the crabs and lobster, caught fresh that morning in the clean waters of the North Sea, or so they claimed at least, and thought perhaps of the parable of the multiplication of the fishes or the water turning into wine. If *that* miracle happened again, it would surely put a smile back on the accountant's face. As if it would have been inappropriate in the hours preceding an exalted visitation, there was no music to be heard anywhere: you heard cutlery scraping over plates, and hushed tones were no longer reserved for gossip. A silent torchlight procession arose spontaneously on the Place de Brouckère. Well, it wasn't just torches, there were also devout people who joined in with nightlights, a candle stub, a smouldering cigar butt . . . scenes that were more usual when yet another filthy murder had forced our society to assuage its impotence with a march. Was this an act of desperation by god-fearing souls who had left it too late to mend their ways? I didn't know how else to interpret it.

That night, for the first time since moving to the city centre, Veronique and I slept with the windows open and I didn't have to lie there watching the red light on the billboard flash over our ceiling at exhausting intervals. I would have sworn that it was a bucolic world, free of exhaust fumes and as quiet as the days before the birth of Henry Ford. (By the way, I couldn't remember the last time I'd heard a siren.)

After this night everything would be different; it was impossible to close your bedroom door with any other thought. Christ was going to reveal Himself to us and we still didn't know why. Maybe to present us with the bill for our lives. Maybe for some other reason. But it seemed obvious that He had plans for us. At the very least, He would have a message for us, and it was highly questionable whether we – genetically only slightly modified apes, after all – were ready for it.

My conscience kept me awake longer than the mosquitoes. I wanted to say 'I love you' to Veronique, because I thought it was what I should say, because I was in a hurry to salvage something. But I didn't believe myself.

(*'Purge me with hyssop, and I shall be clean; wash me, and I shall be whiter than snow.'*)

Thirteenth Station

The afternoon of the twenty-first of July, the day of days, around 2 pm. A more-than-favourable moment to carry out break-ins here and there around the country. Even if that was the furthest thing from anyone's mind. With all means of telecommunication at our disposal, we were trying to get an update on the current situation. Not *one* reliable source could confirm that the Messiah had already arrived in Brussels, but we realised that it was completely out of the question that Christ's precise location at this crucial juncture in the history of Belgium and all of mankind would be released to the general public. On the whole planet, there were at most three or four people who were fully briefed at this moment in time. At least that's what *I* thought, influenced perhaps by a few overly exciting spy films.

★

Veronique and I had abandoned our plan of watching the solemn events on TV after all. A sense of history in the making pushed us out onto the street like everyone else. If you had a chance to see Jesus with your own two eyes, you'd be daft to admire Him through a cameraman's viewfinder. It was elbow work, of course, to lay claim to a spot on the cobbles of the Rue Ducale with a view of the royal box trees; even making it that far was a miracle in itself. We'd aimed for a better spot at first, but that turned out to be reserved for a group of cancer patients. They had lost their faith in science, cancelled all treatment and travelled to Brussels in the hope of being touched by the Hand that once gave light to the blind, birdsong to the deaf and a new lease of life to Lazarus. As a demonstration of their faith in a favourable outcome, a few of them had already planted cigarettes in the middle of their movingly emaciated faces.

The Rue Ducale had to do, and now we were there. Or, as a few of the extremely pricey T-shirts on sale around us proclaimed in English, 'Jesus was in Brussels – the same day as me.'

That's right, we were part of that privileged whole, but when we saw how others had set themselves up on rooftops with telescopes and folding chairs, preferably with a crate of beer, a bag of charcoal and a kilo of lamb chops within reach, we also felt like nothing so much as members of a stupid herd. The art nouveau building of the Old England clothing store on Rue Montagne de la Cour, for some time now home to a musical instrument museum, had opened up its panoramic roof terrace to bring in the punters; the Ferris wheel on the Boulevard Poincaré had hiked its prices but was still full of slick operators with 500-ride tickets, who had been rotating constantly since early in the morning with binoculars and air-sickness bags at the ready. And all of that without any guarantee of success, as there still wasn't an official programme.

From where I was standing I could just make out the tent with the guests of honour – at least, if the man in front of me with the child on his shoulders changed position for a second or two to rest a few muscles. The monarch with his entire household, the provincial governor, the prime minister of the permanent provisional government for business in hand, the politician charged with trying to form a coalition, the politician charged with assessing the likelihood of succeeding in forming a coalition, the politician charged with mediating the formation of the coalition, the politician charged with clarifying the state of the coalition formation . . . As far as I could tell from where I was standing, they all looked fairly relaxed. The King in particular radiated a certain languor – he had a definite air of self-satisfaction, and that inspired confidence in all that was about to happen.

If anything was about to happen.

We scanned the heavens, identifying signs of His imminence in everything that presented itself: a piece of paper floating on the breeze, a pigeon coming in elegantly to land . . . Faith was all we needed, surely, and the seas would part before us.

At quarter to three or thereabouts there was suddenly some action when, despite the general ban on motorised emitters of particulate pollution, a red-and-white-checked 2CV came sputtering up the closed-off circuit. Girls with saucy expressions blew kisses and threw lengths of salami into the crowd, completely free of charge, and these welcome snacks certainly eased the waiting. 'Try it French-style: taste Cochonou *saucisson!*'

Of course – a promotional pageant! There's no such thing as a free lunch, and if it was possible to bankroll the whole event with donations from generous companies, why not? If Christ's festive but expensive visit wasn't necessarily going to imply grit shortages next winter or our rusty lampposts remaining unreplaced alongside our old-fashioned motorways for yet another year, the taxpayers would be wise not to grumble about this spiritual holiday being brought to us with the aid of a contribution from selected capitalists. Look, there was another float filled with hip youngsters, angels of the age of consumerism, tossing white hats into the grasping audience. Sponsored by Skoda: '*voiture officielle du Paradis*'. Shall I admit it? I was so glad to get my hands on one of those hats, I waved it around like a big kid. Because I of course had not thought of protecting myself against the burning sun – or the rays of Christ's halo – before leaving home. Foresight is not one of my strengths. Never has been. But coming down with sunstroke was the last thing I wanted on that day of days.

Other products I remember as gracing the first part of the parade: a host baker, the brewer of a renowned abbey beer (who, unfortunately, failed to provide samples, the stingy bastard), a betting shop, canned olives . . .

The various tourist boards had also realised that a more beautiful opportunity for promoting our country would never arise. The international press had turned out in its entirety with zoom lenses as big as bazookas. The entire planet was going to have images of our country branded on its retinas today, and not because we'd stolen the world endurance record for forming a government from under the nose of the Iraqis. Accordingly, the tourism barons had the clown-like Gilles of Binche marching down the boulevards – and because it was still a long way to go to mandarin season, these carnival characters were tossing Swiss chard, French

beans and turnip greens into the mob as a summer variant
– courtesy of Haspengouw district, where tubers thrive.
From Dendermonde came Bayard the magic horse with four
intellectually challenged children on its saddle, the shrimp
fishermen of East Dunkirk rode past on their draughthorses,
from Liège came the giants Tchantchès, Nanesse and Charle-
magne, followed by the royal stilt-walkers of Merchtem,
the dancing leeks of Tilff, the bicycling brass band of Haneffe
... They all passed by while pamphlets praising our hotel
facilities fluttered down around us.

A wave of mild hysteria swept through the inner city. Finally,
finally ...The screeches of the masses kept coming closer and
we interpreted this as a sign of His presence. And, yes, a divine,
bare-footed figure did come round the corner with the
cheering, dressed in white robes, shining like photographic
paper, inadvertently stepping in the pies left behind by the
shrimper's horses. But it was an actor from the Nieuwkerk
theatrical society The Flax Flower, most recent winner of
the National Theatre Prize, in the role of his life. Various key
scenes from Jesus's life were acted out for us according
to medieval theatrical conventions, as if to refresh our
knowledge of the catechism before He Himself put in an
appearance. The annunciation, the manger in Bethlehem,

driving the money changers out of the temple, the betrayal by Judas, the story of Barabbas, the crucifixion, the whole kit and caboodle . . . The guy playing Joseph wasn't bad at all, I thought. The role of Pontius Pilate was filled excellently too. A man with the perfect face for the part. But we hadn't over-populated this city to admire street theatre and pageant plays. People were still keeping it under their breath for now, but the grumbling was swelling. If it hadn't been for the sight of the King up on stage flossing a remnant of Cochonou sausage out from between two teeth with an expression that didn't betray the slightest sign of unease, we wouldn't have tired our legs any longer.

The next part of the caravan could lay claim to a more concrete link to the announced entry of our most welcome guest. A parade of penitent criminals – serious offenders, murderers from the prisons of Lantin, Hasselt and Merksplas – marched down the street unshackled, without so much as an ankle bracelet between them. Begging for public humili-ation from the flabbergasted viewers, crawling for forgiveness. We recognised a gangster boss, an escape artist, an infamous paedophile, the jealous wife who provided the clientele of our hairdressing salons with weeks of entertaining discussions by castrating her adulterous husband with a paring knife. If the people had wanted to take revenge on these sinners with all the blind, mindless power of the mob, they could have done so easily and the malefactors' innards would have been splattered over the ground in no time. But how insignificant was our rage compared with the Judgment that lay ahead for these lost sheep? The Righteous One was approaching. If not for the fact that He was probably as scentless as a new-born deer, we could have smelt Him already, truly, so close was He now.

Even more pathetic were the guilty who came in the wake of the official criminals. These were poor wretches *without* a record, respectable citizens whose lives had deviated only slightly from the straight and narrow: a banker, a vendor of affordable dreams that had pushed many to bankruptcy; a property speculator; a stockbroker; the boss of a factory who paid his employees a pittance and drove them like slaves. But also a mother who thought she had neglected her children; an alcoholic husband with a quick temper and a slow wife; a forty-something having an affair with the woman next door; a mechanic who knew which customers you could con about the state of the engine and which ones you couldn't . . . the whole gamut of minor sinners. I saw my upstairs neighbour, Antoine — yes, of course, I should have expected that. I saw Antoine and called out his name, inappropriate as it was, as happy as a toddler, proud to have recognised someone who was playing a role in this historic event. But Antoine kept his eyes hellbound. Humble. Some of the marchers flagellated their backs to shreds with whips, others pounded nails into their flesh. No, it wasn't tasteful. And by the time I saw a section of this penitential procession turning their tongues raw and bloody by licking the cobblestones clean, I really was sick of this show of self-chastisement.

Someone had apparently read my mind, because all this misery came to an abrupt end in the form of a float with worshipful wenches. There couldn't have been a more glaring contrast. An array of rows and rows of teeth exposed in gleaming smiles, cleaned with Fluoracil toothpaste – waving hands, coquettish gestures, plastic faces. Miss Belgium, Miss Shopping Flanders, Miss Sports Belgium, the Strawberry Princess, the Grape Queen, the winner of The Most Beautiful Female Farmer in Flanders, the Oak Queen, Miss Chocolate, Miss Dender, Miss Diamond and Miss Tractor-Pulling (the last-mentioned was seated on the tractor that was pulling the float with her colleagues on board – the organisers certainly had an eye for detail!). I could think of more beautiful things, even people, to illustrate the magnificence of Creation, but it seemed impossible that this motorised meat market could have been intended for any other purpose.

That year's Miss Asparagus had overslept and came limping after her trailer on a broken stiletto, thus winning for herself the honour of bringing this curtain-raiser to a close.

At least, I call it a 'curtain-raiser' now . . .

For a good half hour after the passage of the – naturally – blonde ambassadress of asparagus nothing happened. Then a column of the motorised unit of the Royal Guard appeared and we knew things were getting serious. Flashing lights. Mercedeses. Giants with armour-plated chests in tailor-made suits, gleaming with sweat, focused. Even more Mercedeses. Only now did the tension rise to a maximum. The heat wasn't helping and the long, motionless wait will have had an equally deleterious influence. More than one good soul couldn't bear another second and collapsed unconscious. To the well-concealed delight of those around them, who gained both breathing space and an improved view. All this fuss was caused by the appearance of the little girl Ohanna, dressed ceremonially as a communicant. That is, she was dressed the way my parents were dressed for *their* First Holy Communion. If I'm not mistaken, nowadays children take their oath of religiosity in jeans, pulled up or sagging, as the case may be. I mean, the rare children who still see the inside of a church. The bodyguards were hard put to protect the girl from all-too-pushy pilgrims. Ohanna had a link to the Prophet, inspired columnists had dared to describe her as the first apostlette, an extension of both the Lord and of His Word. Yes, one wasn't shy of an archaism more or less. All frills were allowed in these hours. But because Ohanna's status had been written up to such heights, some readers had become convinced that she was on the same level as the Nazarene. Seeing her walking there like that reminded me, and not just me, of Nepal's Kumaris, young girls of fourteen at most who have been recognised as reincarnations of the Hindu goddess Durga. They are worshipped and get a horrible existence in return. Their lives are no longer theirs, but the masses'. And with the same logic, hysterical gangs now wanted to touch Ohanna. Photos of sick relatives were held out for her to kiss. Open suppurating words were bared before her, one touch of her hand would suffice. Flowers were pressed upon her. Along with artificial limbs as tokens of thanks for so-called miraculous cures. One person wanted to dab her forehead with a hankie, another devotee wanted to wash her feet and cut her nails. As I said, the security men had their hands full. It cost them blood, sweat and tears to get Ohanna up to the seats of honour on the stage. But they did it.

She sat down next to the King.

Silence descended over Brussels.

Now there was only one Person left for Whom we were waiting.

Fourteenth Station

As a community, we could easily have reacted differently. I would have found it far preferable if, on arriving at that point of realisation, we'd all burst out laughing. A giggling fit rising up over the whole city centre, tireless laughter gurgling out of hundreds of thousands of mouths for hours on end. Sometimes I still dream of that missed opportunity, us slapping our thighs on the evening of that twenty-first day of July, at the hour when all hopes had been dashed, rolling over the ground and shrieking with pure delight at having let ourselves be taken for such a massive ride. Christ hadn't come, hallelujah! Hello? You could hardly call it a surprise. But what was so immensely funny about it was that we, invariably practical, sceptical, bone-dry hyperrealists that we were, had so looked forward to His coming. We had infected each other with enthusiasm preparing ourselves for a day that we, in the essence of our being, were incapable of believing in. The joke of the century: collectively we had expected salvation and that salvation had to come from somewhere else.

We should have pissed ourselves laughing, nothing else would have done.

The joke of the century, yep. But getting it required a talent for self-mockery and an ability to see the bigger picture. It was true that we had once been the proud owners of these pleasant traits, but no-one could convince me they hadn't been lost somewhere along the way. It was indisputable – we'd been led by the nose in an excellent practical joke and responded by choosing the worst of all possible scenarios: we swallowed our defeat humourlessly and crawled back behind our withered façades.

When two gendarmes grabbed little Ohanna by the arms, we realised all too well what was going to happen: today, or tomorrow at the latest, she'd be on a plane, despite the government's earlier promises. We didn't protest. After all, we had put our everyday death masks back on and resumed the role that fitted us like a second skin: indifference.

There was no room for doubt; everywhere the flower-boxes were being lugged back inside out of fear of itching delinquent fingers, the fronts of the buildings had taken on their familiar grey, our view contracted once again to satellite dishes, peeling paint and tiny balconies with rusty wrought iron and crumbling concrete. We turned the faces we had been showing each other for almost three weeks back to the ground as if we would find our future destinations there and nowhere else.

The sounds of sirens and impatient, blasting car horns had returned with a vengeance.

All of a sudden I caught a glimpse of the policeman with the enormous birthmark on his face, and he didn't seem at all consoled by the reassurance of ongoing job opportunities in the police force. He was stressed and couldn't hide it. Brussels had been living a lie; it had been a pleasant lie, but a lie for all that, and now the city was getting back to reality. A more resolute return to business as usual was harder to imagine than the one provided by several, some would almost say classic, riots in the Rue de Ribaucourt, caused by boys who had only just sprouted moustaches. Convinced that they needed to brighten the emptiness of their lives with the cling-clang of a few shop windows, they were also clever enough to legitimise their vicious misbehaviour with a sense of discrimination. A number 75 bus was destroyed in the neighbourhood of Bizet for the pleasure of destruction, and it was definitely not the first and definitely not the last either. On route 46 a bus driver was dragged out of his cabin before having his face 'adjusted' with a baseball bat. Simply because the unfortunate driver had been impertinent enough to ask a passenger for his ticket. We knew how those conversations went. 'What? My ticket? Do I look like a fare dodger to you? Is that what you're trying to say? That I'm not respectable enough for your standards of etiquette? That I don't care about the rules and want to ride for free? You'd already judged me before I got on your shitty bus . . .'

He'd been able to rest his vocal cords for quite a while now, but the Brussels police spokesman was soon running short of saliva once again.

Of course, nowadays everyone denies ever putting a scrap of faith in the communiqué about the miraculous entry. 'Christ coming to Brussels? And Tutankhamen to Antwerp, I suppose?' You know the kind of thing: they were standing there in the inner city with hundreds of thousands of others waiting for the arrival of an air bubble just for the festive occasion, attending the non-event for its own sake, a bit of fun. Still, you'll just have to take my word for it when I say I never had any faith in God to lose. As a consequence, I can't claim to be devastated by the cancellation of His coming. If I'd begun to believe in anything during those days, it was that I was finally allowed to live somewhere where people looked each other in the eye when their paths crossed. Where you didn't have to be an egotistical slimeball to secure a seat on a tram. Where people didn't walk past a beggar in exactly the same way they walked past a parking meter. That our short and simple existences had at least a shred of significance for each other. That was the most painful thing: realising that I had been so keen to delude myself about human nature like that.

Veronique didn't speak for a long time walking home that evening, but I had a feeling one of her famous moods was brewing. She undoubtedly blamed me personally for us having stayed in Brussels this summer. Soon her holidays would be over and she wouldn't have had an opportunity to recharge her batteries in any way at all. Now I just had to wait until the next row, undoubtedly set off by something completely banal, and she would succumb to the temptation to throw it all in my face. My idiotic idea of not going away on holiday. My idea to associate with murderous neighbours. My idea and not hers to dedicate our few days off to a supposedly transcendental experience we would share with the masses, losing ourselves in solidarity with an antisocial mob.

★

We'd taken the tram – the packed tram, because everybody had hit on the plan of getting away from the centre of the capital as quickly as possible – and it was one of the last things Veronique and I would do as a couple. We knew that. We felt it. It had been in the air for months.

The commuters' faces were the kind of faces you'd see any day in February. Or November. A rainy day. As if we had all completed the umpteenth joyless week of work and there was no promise of any happiness in the weekend that had just started. Or as if we hadn't completed a single day of work for the simple reason that we couldn't get a job. Travellers gripped their bags tightly, staring out of the windows or at their own reflections. A few fled this dismalness along the usual escape route, texting moderately funny messages that might be read on another tram, in the same dismalness.

'*Il faut s'oublier pour révéler sa vraie beauté,*' a young woman had suddenly said, looking up from a book whose title I was unfortunately unable to read. She shook all those beautiful words up in her head, as if in a snowdome, then stared at them as they slowly began their descent. I think I was jealous of her, because I, like all the others, had lost the courage to say something of beauty out loud. Everyone was looking at her, but not openly, only sideways, surreptitiously, disapprovingly. Some of them employed their hairstyles the way gossips in rural hamlets use curtains. But even before the young woman's words had time to come back to rest, she was addressed (someone was speaking to someone else!) by an odious character – a sour herring, who I won't deign to describe further, even if he was ugly enough to make it easy for me – who growled in Flemish, 'I don't know if you realise it girlie, but this is Brussels, huh? Keep your French to yourself!'

She got off at Étangs Noirs, the subway station with the most beautiful name, *black ponds*, and I'm inclined to believe that alone was the reason she left the vehicle there. Étangs Noirs, where the escalator had been broken for months and the malcontents needed regular announcements to remind them of the possibility of lifting up their own feet for a change. It was only in my thoughts that I followed her. I was too much of a coward to live. Too chicken–shit to be the god of my own hours.

Pilate answered, 'What I have written, I have written.'

John 19:22